About the Author

Robert Russin has always preferred the imaginary world of stories compared to the linear grind of accounting and auditing. Like all others, he has wondered what the afterlife is like. *Light Burns* is his interpretation of that life. He likes the expanse of the desert and the force of a summer thunderstorm. He is a member of the Ahwatukee Writers Group, whose guidance has been invaluable.

Light Burns

Robert Russin

Light Burns

Olympia Publishers
London

www.olympiapublishers.com
OLYMPIA PAPERBACK EDITION

Copyright © Robert Russin 2023

The right of Robert Russin to be identified as author of
this work has been asserted in accordance with sections 77 and 78 of
the Copyright, Designs and Patents Act 1988.

All Rights Reserved

No reproduction, copy or transmission of this publication
may be made without written permission.
No paragraph of this publication may be reproduced,
copied or transmitted save with the written permission of the publisher,
or in accordance with the provisions
of the Copyright Act 1956 (as amended).

Any person who commits any unauthorized act in relation to
this publication may be liable to criminal
prosecution and civil claims for damage.

A CIP catalogue record for this title is
available from the British Library.

ISBN: 978-1-80439-056-6

This is a work of fiction.
Names, characters, places and incidents originate from the writer's
imagination. Any resemblance to actual persons, living or dead, is
purely coincidental.

First Published in 2023

Olympia Publishers
Tallis House
2 Tallis Street
London
EC4Y 0AB

Printed in Great Britain

Dedication

To my Sweeter who has seen me at my best and at my worst.

Acknowledgements

Many persons of the Ahwatukee Writers Group gave me guidance but four persons deserve special recognition. Thank you Victoria Garrison, Ed Prestwood, Andy Wolfendon, and Katana McDaniel. Recognition also goes to Jean Claude Baker and Chris Chase, authors of Josephine – The Hungry Heart. Start here to begin your search for the earthly life of Josephine Baker.

Chapter 1

Nothing is destroyed. It only changes form.

Where did this thought come from? Maybe I heard it from my science teacher Mr. Ferguson back in high school. Perhaps I read about it on the Internet, or maybe I read it in passing. Anyway, it was bouncing around my brain as I waited for the cashier to process my payment.

"Wheedle-lee-deet, wheedle-lee-deet," the card reader chirped. The printed screen said, 'PLEASE REMOVE CARD' in black print. I put the card back in a sleeve of my purse. "Thank you, please come again." The cashier smiled and gave me my receipt. The unnatural chill gave the grocery store a sterile, empty scent as I headed toward the door.

Storm clouds were on the horizon as I wheeled the grocery cart out of the store. A wheel squeaked as I entered the parking lot and headed for the car. Angled white parking stripes glared in the sticky heat. The overhead sun was blistering as it colluded with a soggy breeze coming from the south, riffling the grocery bags. I wiped some sweat off my face to get a fleeting moment of comfort before putting on my sunglasses.

"Hi, Dawn." Becky crossed the space between the parking lot and the grocery store, looking like she was enjoying the cool pines of Flagstaff. She was wearing a pair of tight white shorts and a maroon University of Oklahoma t-shirt, which was definitely a size too small. I called it her 'I'm looking for a man' outfit. Other women would have called it her 'I want to show you a good time' outfit or worse. We had been friends since elementary school, getting in and out of trouble while getting good grades. High school came where she said in the girl's locker room white shorts were important because it made boys think she was a virgin. I remember when she applied lipstick, smiled into the mirror and said she liked to make them try. After high school, we went our separate ways, she to the University of Oklahoma and me to Northern Arizona University. Now she worked in public relations while I owned a running store called *The Running Phoenix*.

"Becky, so good to see you." I sensed we were about to go on another adventure.

"What have you been doing lately?" Sweat seemed to stay away from her, as if she had waterproof skin.

A fleeting rush of heat passed through me. "Tonight, I will cook for Tom."

Becky gave a dirty smile, and one of her eyes blinked. "Really, he must be special if you will cook for him."

Did she just wink at me? I returned a cleaner smile and said, "He is."

"How long has it been?"

My heart thumped a little faster when I heard myself say, "six months." The grocery bags contained his favorites, perhaps every man's favorites: hamburgers, fries, beer, onions, pickles, lemon meringue pie, and chocolate ice cream. At the top of one bag was a jar of hot mustard. My feelings for Tom and the first decent week for my business put a bounce into my step. Nonstop customers all week resulting in $36,000 in gross revenues and it happened in late July, the slowest time of the year. All the planning and preparation finally showed signs of paying off. The lack of customers from the disastrous Fourth of July weekend was a distant memory. I could not wait for the snowbirds to arrive in October.

"Wow!" Becky's eyelids opened to reveal chestnut brown eyes, which she knew how to use.

"How about you, anything new?" I asked.

"Just work really, the hours in public relations get crazy."

"I'm sure it is. Hey, I have to go. The ice cream is melting."

"Sure, I'll catch you later," Becky said as we turned away. A breeze ruffled the grocery bags as I proceeded to the parking lot. My armpits sent me a whiff of body odor as I wiped off more sweat. I ignored the distant storm clouds moving east toward the White Mountains and the New Mexico state line. Living in Phoenix meant someone else got the rain. Suddenly, a white light encased me and my teeth clamped shut. My hands gripped the grocery cart and my face locked into place. My sight went black before slowly coming back into focus. People ran around parked cars to hover around a shape lying amid the parking stripes. I joined them and found my body lying on the pavement; the shirt scorched, my hair and neck showing burns and shredded skin. Terror invaded me as I realized something separated me from my life.

"No!" I shouted, wondering what to do.

"That lightning bolt hit her square on. She never knew what hit her," A stranger at my body announced.

My brain fought to regain my life and make sense of my sudden death. *How could a lightning bolt hit me when the storm clouds were so far away? Why didn't I hear the sound?* Becky arrived and started rocking my body as the stranger watched. "Oh my God! Oh my God! Oh my God!" she repeated as panic filled her brown eyes.

I rushed toward my body, darting between the legs of a man,

and tried to get back in and continue my life.

To my horror, the skin of my body slowly changed color on the hot pavement. The burns on my shredded shirt looked like an iron charred it and my neck had a spider-web pattern that gave off a smell of burned flesh. More people closed in as panic washed through me. Another stranger arriving at my body pointed somewhere to the south and said the lightning bolt came from that cloud. His blue cap had gold letters, but I was too busy trying to save myself to read the words.

I found myself back in my body and looked at skin cells, hair cells, nerve cells, and blood platelets. A scream parted from my lips as I left my body, and confusion beset me. Seeing it as I normally would, my hand passed through my body's arm when I tried to touch it. A lilting voice in the crowd said, "She's dead."

"Oh my God, Dawn! No! Oh my God! Oh my God!" Becky panted and her panicked eyes cried as she kept rocking my body.

A man stepped out of the crowd, moved Becky aside, and breathed into my body's mouth. My body's lungs expanded and contracted with every breath he gave, but I sensed everything slipping away. A creeping sense of the unknown advanced and a vision of rowing to the safety of a riverbank as the current pushed me toward the waterfall encroached. The man moved to my body's chest and repeatedly compressed it until a man and woman in uniform arrived with their equipment. My hopes picked up, paramedics.

I searched inside my body to find something that would restore activity to the inert blood, veins, nerves, and tissue. My body's heart shook, looking like it forgot how to pump blood.

The paramedics looked in my body's eyes and said things I partially understood as the smell of burned flesh persisted. They cut off my shirt and bra, which revealed the spider web pattern had reached my breasts. One paramedic took out two paddles, applied a gel and placed them on my chest.

I'm not a woman any more.

"Clear."

A whine came from somewhere and my body heaved. She tried again.

"Clear." It heaved again. "I have a pulse." It was the last words I heard before I entered a black void. I perceived myself floating in a space lacking edges, corners, or depth. It was like being placed into a dreamless trance, and I had no sense how long it lasted. Without warning, light poured in and the void lifted, showing my body again but now in a sterile room of stainless steel, white tile, and an antiseptic odor. People in green gowns and masked faces surrounded my inert body. One of them pressed paddles against my chest, the metal underside glinting off a fluorescent light. A whine filled the room and my body heaved again. She stopped, put them aside, and stepped away.

"Time of death: two thirty p.m.," a doctor pronounced while another man, probably an intern, threw a sheet over my body.

"How sad, such a beautiful woman," one of them said before leaving.

Time of death. What did they mean by that? My body's pupils were cloudy and parts of my body's skin took on a reddish-blue color.

There has to be a mistake. The first flutters of fear arrived as I tried again to rejoin my body, but as I entered, I could see nothing move. Fear rose and a scream mixed with tears as I kept searching for a way to restart my body, but it continued to decay as the minutes and hours passed. Finally, a doctor came in with a middle-aged man and woman wearing street clothes familiar to me. It was my parents, and they approached the table with a sense of dread. The doctor slowly lifted the sheet away from my body's face.

"That's our daughter," my father said as the sight of my body's face paralyzed his eyes, and Mom broke down sobbing.

"Mom, Dad, I'm alive," I yelled but, they did not hear me. Tears came as I yelled louder, "I'm right here!" Still no effect. I yelled to the point of screaming but they did not respond and my sobbing choked back my voice. They then talked about me.

The doctor's voice was neutral. "Because of her age, we need to examine her to rule out a homicide. However, judging by her skin, I would say the injuries she suffered would be consistent with a lightning strike."

"I understand," Dad said. "Can you do it in a way that she can be…" His voice hitched before he continued, "…Presentable?"

"You're not cutting her," Mom shouted and grabbed Dad's arm.

"Mom!" I screamed.

"Rita, we do not have a choice." Dad's face tightened before he yanked his arm from her grip.

"Nobody's cutting my girl." The veins in Mom's neck stood out.

"Doctor, can you give us a few minutes?" Dad asked.

"I'll wait outside." The doctor stepped out, his black shoes squeaking with each step.

"Don't you get it? When he cuts her, she's gone for good." Mom's eyes had the look of a captured animal.

"Rita, our girl's gone already. Look at her. Her lips are blue and her joints are stiff." He touched my body and wept.

Mom pushed him aside, grabbed my body and said through the tears, "Dawn, you need to come back now."

I was a few feet away, but my body's mortal wounds blocked any way back. I tried to say 'goodbye, Mom' but the words' grip was too tight for my throat.

Dad and Mom squared off and argued fiercely, but slowly he wore her down like sand against rock. At last, she gave in and allowed him to call the doctor back.

The doctor returned, shoes squeaking all the way back, and said they would treat me respectfully, saying each word carefully as if laying bricks.

"She must have meant a lot to you," he said.

"You don't know the half of it," her bitter voice retorted.

"No, I don't." He paused before continuing. "Do you have any further questions?"

"I need to say goodbye to my girl," Mom replied through clenched teeth.

"Sure, I will be outside." He left again, shoes squeaking.

Mom and Dad looked at my sheet-covered body, the face exposed. Mom took a brush out of her purse and began brushing my body's hair.

"I remember brushing your hair when you were a little girl. I always liked to brush it and brush it, until it was nice and bright," she said. Tears slipped down her face, some of which hit the face of my body as she kept brushing. "I remember that special Easter day when I brushed your hair. You wore a yellow dress, and I knew you would become a beautiful woman." She went silent and kept brushing and it continued on for so long I thought the doctor would return and stop her, but she stopped. She put the brush back in her purse, took out some lipstick and applied it to the blue lips. "There, that's the right shade for you," she said. She put the lipstick back in her purse, turned her head to Dad and said with a steely voice, "We must make funeral arrangements."

"Yes, we do," he said.

"Don't leave me!" I shrieked.

They called the doctor back in, thanked him for his time, and left me. I wanted to stop them, but I could not leave my body. A brown clipboard lay on the desk, and I read the sheet showing the last entry of my life.

Last Name: Allegary

First Name: Dawn

Date of Death: 12 August 2014

Time of Death: Two thirty p.m.

There were other details about the end of my life, but I could not stand reading them. I already knew the date of my birth, 23 July 1985, which meant I barely got past my twenty-ninth birthday. Out of the corner of my eye, I thought I saw a flash of light, but saw only the stale white light of the fluorescent bulb.

Two men wearing hospital greens entered the room.

"So, this is Dawn, courtesy of a lightning strike," one man said.

The second man pointed at my body. "It must have been quite a shock. I guess she's amped up for the afterlife."

"Ha! Ha! Ha! Ha! Ha!" they laughed.

I died, and the world is making jokes about it. The end of my life truly sucked.

The first man gazed at my butt. "Busted her a new one," he said. They removed the sheet, photographed my stiff body and marked it with a magic marker. They brought tools out, and I understood I would be gone once they cut me. I attacked, but passed through them. Again I attacked, but with the same fruitless result. An older man with white hair and wearing a white coat entered the room. He brought down a microphone, briefly examined my external wounds, and said something into the microphone. He picked up a scalpel from the tray and I watched the edge of my life quickly leave my sight as he took apart the creation that was me on a sterile, lifeless stainless-steel table. The creation, which took a few minutes of conception, nine months of pregnancy, and endless hours of nurturing to adulthood, gone. I screamed, and everything became a blur.

I found myself outside the hospital under some flowers. The flowers' sweet fragrance did nothing to relieve the tears, loneliness, and fear that buried me. Eventually the tears stopped, and I looked around.

People came and went. The hospital windows stood flush inside their squares, but everything looked different. The street nearby was still Frye Boulevard, but it looked larger, wider and taller. *Wait, I'm too tall to be under a flower.* The petals looked like large awnings and its sweet odor engulfed me. I discovered myself floating and giving off a hard pulsating brown and black light. *What happened to me?* I touched my face. *What do I look like?* I peeked through the petals again and saw silhouettes of bushes, trees, and other plants emitting solitary lights of green and brown. Flowers radiated hues of orange, yellow, purple, pink, and red, drifting by as if floating down a lazy river. Some of these plants looked familiar, but others looked foreign. A bush came close, surprising me, but drifted away. *God, I'm in trouble!* Did I call for God out of my own free will or did some other part of me intervene? I had not thought of God since my Sunday school days. My brain divided with one part trying to figure out how to survive; and the other part trying to figure out why I lost my life buying groceries. It bounced between these two problems until it heard a noise. A silhouette came into view, floated above the ground, and gave off a dominant indigo glow followed by a lesser orange light. It had a question mark tail, and from the stripes I deduced it was a tabby. The cat looked straight at me and gave a paper shredder "Meow." The sound filled my ears as the cat rubbed against my leg. A flash caught the corner of my eye. My head jerked, and another silhouette appeared. She radiated a strong, blue and green light. Her silhouette was a mix of ebony, ivory, and long legs. "I see you have met Tourner," she said.

"You're a ghost!" I gasped, and a frigid chill gripped me. She looked me in the eye and said, "No, I'm a woman and my name is Josephine." Two thick black bands covered her reproductive organs. I glanced down and found I also had two bands. "What happened to my breasts?" My voice rose.

"Just reach under your shade." I reached inside and breathed a sigh of relief of when I touched the familiar feminine curves. The spider web pattern was not there. I was a woman again. "Your girls are safe and sound. Now what's your name?"

"Dawn." Sunlight flashed out of a cloud, partially obscuring my sight.

"Hi, Dawn, welcome to the eternal life." A smile spread out.

"The what?" I asked.

"The eternal life, you know it as the afterlife. What caused you to pass through?"

"Pass through?"

"We refer to people who died as passing through as opposed to passing away." The sun passed behind another cloud and a bee the size of a golf ball passed by me with wings whirring, causing me to flinch. "They said lightning struck me."

"That'll do it."

My lights were still pulsating."

"What's become of me?" I stammered.

"Your appearance has changed. You look similar to me. Your

colors show your emotions. Brown means you're having trouble making sense of things; black means you're trying to protect yourself. They're vibrating because you're frightened."

My face crunched up, but I held back my tears.

"There, there, Dawn. I'll help you through." Her hand reached for me, but I retreated.

"Who are you?" My hands clenched and rose. Josephine stepped back and showed me her brown eyes.

"I'm a searcher. We search for the people who passed through and help them adjust to the eternal life. Our society has been around for centuries." I just looked at her. "I know you just died, and everything has changed and now this strange-looking woman comes along with a cat." She broke into a smile so wide it looked like it could contain the Grand Canyon. "Let me tell you about the eternal life." My thoughts jumped at the chance to make sense of all this, but another part of me remained wary. Was she good or was she evil? A man wearing blue coveralls pushed an old woman crumpled in a wheelchair through the entrance door. "Now Dawn, do you want to come out here and join me or do you want to spend your eternal life hiding in the flowers?" Keeping my eyes on her, I emerged from the petals. I saw Tourner's bright glow and asked if all animals come to the eternal life. "All creation passes to the eternal life. Now, do I have your attention?" My eyes stayed locked onto her.

"Yes." Josephine told me my previous existence was in the earthly life, but the earthly life ends. She showed me I passed through, but I continued to live.

"Are you with me so far?" I nodded. "You asked what became of you. The silhouette made you alive in the earthly life and it came with you when you passed through because it is part of your eternal life. Your body did not pass through because it is part of the earthly life. However, you're still Dawn, even though you physically changed." The light slowly steadied as I calmed down.

"I have a silhouette?"

"Are you ready to see it?" She sounded like she was offering me a present.

"Yes," I replied timidly.

"Then let's find a friendly place to show you." The smile returned and beckoned me to follow. My parents' warnings about strangers blared, but I followed her, anyway. "

Where are we going?" I asked.

"We need to find a mirror." We left, but I kept Josephine and Tourner in front of me. Josephine and Tourner crossed Frye Boulevard, oblivious to an oncoming car. My mouth opened, but no words came out as the car passed through them without effect. Josephine turned around and waited for me. The light changed and after I crossed; she laughed.

"Why weren't you hurt?" I asked.

"You wanted to see me hurt?" she said.

"No, but that car passed through you."

"The car is in the earthly life. You don't have to wait for traffic lights any more."

"So the car would have no effect on me if I stepped out in front of it?"

"You observed what I just did." A pickup truck with its grill gleaming and its engine humming approached. I picked out a spot in the road just to my left. The windshield, rear-view mirror, and driver got larger as the truck got closer. Sensing it would splat me like a bug, I rushed back to the curb, and the truck passed by with a growl. "You'll do it, eventually," Josephine said.

"It seems like suicide." We came to a house with faded rose

bricks and a half open curtain inviting us to look. Purple and yellow flowers and short black lights bordered a walkway which led around a corner. We followed the path to a porch which had an enormous wood door and a doorknob as large as a baseball. "Josephine, how are we going to enter? Do you have a key?" She smiled.

"We are going through the door."

"We will kick it down?"

"No, we're not capable of doing that." She kept on smiling.

"Are we going to wait until someone opens the door?"

"No, we will not wait. Follow me." Without waiting for me, she disappeared into the door, leaving me dumbfounded. She reappeared, popping out of the wood grain like a bubble.

"Well, are you going to follow me?"

I just looked at the door.

"Dawn, you're in the eternal life now. You can go through this door." I expected the wood to resist my touch, but I went in. A sense of drowning washed over me as I found myself among the fibers making up the grain. I screamed, rushed out the door and back onto the porch. Josephine and Tourner reappeared. "Let's try this again," she said.

"Let's not."

"You'll find it difficult to get around if you don't learn this."

"Okay," I mumbled.

"Now get close behind me, trust me, and follow me."

I tensed up but followed her, anyway. The door was full of fibers and holes and I was sure we would become lost, but we exited and entered a room with an odor of stale air. "Now, that wasn't so bad," Josephine said airily.

"What do you mean not so bad? I passed through a door and a car passed through you."

"Dawn, you're trying to apply your experience in the earthly life to the eternal life."

"It's not making any sense."

"It will take some time to adjust." She paused. "Are you ready to face the mirror?"

"I don't know." The silence became more and more uncomfortable as we just stood there until I finally said, "Okay, let's see what I look like."

"Remember, don't compare what you see in the mirror to the earthly life." I followed her to a bedroom which contained a queen-size bed, a dresser, a mirror, a lamp, and shag carpeting. Gray dust inundated the carpet fibers, which looked and smelled disgusting. "Why does everything appear so large?" I asked.

"To answer your question, we'll need the mirror." A man entered, filling me with fright.

"Josephine, we must get out of here before they arrest us." She laughed hard and long enough to make me twitch and squirm. "Josephine, contain yourself, the man will hear you." I looked away as the man stripped to his underwear and pulled out a pair of blue shorts and a black shirt from the dresser. Josephine laughed even harder before it finally died down in fits and starts, like a bicycle with sticking brakes.

"Dawn, if you're like this in the eternal life, I'll be laughing until eternity ends. Arrested, are you serious? The police do not arrest what they cannot see or hear." She laughed some more. Seeing him dressed, I asked Josephine why the man didn't notice us. "The sounds we emit are too low to for him to hear us and we're too small for him to see us. Now are you ready?"

"Yes." I trembled.

"Well, do it." I took a deep breath, looked into the glass, and gasped at my reflection. The mirror showed an ivory silhouette smaller than a pinpoint giving off a bruised brown and black glow; the brown being dominant and the black bands Josephine called 'the shade' circled my breasts and crotch. My face no longer had lines and blemishes, and my thumb no longer had a scar. The man's reflection filled the mirror.

"My thumb had a scar when I cut it with a kitchen knife," I said.

"You have a brand new body now."

The brown and black flashed again. "Why is my light bruised?"

"You died an untimely death," Josephine said with a neutral voice. The words 'untimely death' made me shudder, and my reflection made me seem smaller. "You'll get messed up if you keep comparing what you are now to what you were." She sounded like my Fourth grade teacher, the one I got in trouble with when she caught me pulling the fire alarm.

"But the earthly life is all I've ever known."

"Well, you will have to make a change," she barked. It took a while, but the light stopped flashing. A brief silence, Josephine said, "We must stop for a while. I have to work, but before we stop, I have a question for you." My silhouette jerked.

"A question?"

"That's right, a question." She squared her silhouette and looked me in the eye. "How would you like a second chance?" Her question was like a life preserver thrown to a drowning man.

"I'm going back?"

"You know it doesn't work that way," she said.

Despair and anger crashed my hopes. "Don't play games with me."

Josephine's voice rose. "I'm not playing games with you. You have a second chance called the eternal life, but you only get one." She moved back a step. "Now I have to go to work."

"There's work in the eternal life?"

"Yes, the eternal life has work. You can come with me or you can wait here." I caught a whiff of the shag carpeting, saw the thick dirt and went with her.

"One more thing," Josephine said. "Look at the man."

I did so.

"They stand. We float."

We left the room and returned to the street with Tourner leading. The summer heat kept everyone inside as we passed each house. Water arced from a sprinkler onto grass and sidewalk. I was about to move closer to Tourner when Josephine stopped me. "Give him room, he's searching."

"Searching for what?"

"He's searching for the recently passed through like you." Tourner's eyes looked everywhere as we moved down the street. My eyes tired with boredom after watching him for a few minutes, but Josephine observed everything. Aware that I did not know if she was good or evil, I asked her a question.

"So, what does a searcher do?" I asked.

"We seek people who have no one to meet them when they pass through." Her eyes kept moving. *None of my relatives were there for me.* My black light became equally dominant with my brown light as they flashed again. "Uh oh, you're having issues." There was that teacher's voice again.

"I didn't say anything." My voice sounded like a lie.

"Dawn, I've been doing this for a long time." Her eyes gave me a look saying, "Don't try me."

"Why didn't my grandmother or any of my relatives come for me?" Her hand waved at me for a second and stopped.

"Wait a minute, when did your grandmother die?"

It was the day I learned there was death. "It was 13 June 1992."

"And what's today's date?"

"12 August 2014."

"Your grandmother had to keep living. Did you really expect her to wait for you to pass through?" Josephine acted as if I should have known it. I admitted to myself she had a point, as twenty-two years had passed.

"Is she still around?"

"She's around, but the hard part will be to find her. The eternal life is an enormous place." Her eyes kept searching. I wondered where she was and what she had been doing. Memories of other relatives appeared, Grandfather, Uncle Joe and Aunt Beatrice. A pale yellow light joined my brown and black lights as I felt a sense of urgency.

"I want to find her." Josephine did not respond, and the silence returned. Tourner kept searching, and I kept thinking about my relatives as cars and trucks drove by. A flash of sunlight caught my eye as it emerged from behind some other clouds. Itching to talk, I asked her about her past. "So how did you live your earthly life?" I asked.

"I was in show business." Her blue and green glow increased like a flame finding extra fuel. "I was the name which was so big they gave me two funerals." My thoughts jarred as if hitting a bump in the road. Who gets two funerals? A thought of my funeral surfaced, but I pushed it away.

"When did you have these funerals?" My voice flattened as I tried to play it cool.

"1975."

"Two funerals, that's impressive." My voice went flatter.

"You don't believe me." Josephine's voice carried a sharp

edge.

"Why wouldn't I believe you?"

"Don't mess with me." Her light changed to a vicious red, pushing down the blue and green lights.

Two funerals, nobody gets two funerals. My mouth moved to make a sarcastic comment but stopped because this potentially dangerous woman knew how to navigate this unfamiliar world. "Sorry, no intent to be disrespectful, I just don't know." My voice returned to normal, but I noted that red meant angry.

Josephine's vicious red evaporated and the blue and green lights returned to Josephine's silhouette, which I associated with calm. "Apology accepted."

We came to an intersection with green and white street signs saying Hazlett and Dawson streets. We turned on Dawson Street, revealing the hospital was about a mile away. The sun bounced its harsh light off its gray-white slab, which towered over the adjacent neighborhoods. A bright white thunderhead dominated the horizon, moving east toward New Mexico. The winds inside would toss the brownish-white dust, and silver ribbons of rain would fall to earth. Living in Phoenix, someone else got the rain. Tourner continued searching, and I returned to thinking about my relatives, but the quiet did not last long as Josephine tossed the question back. "So, how did you live your earthly life?" She said it like a schoolyard bully.

"I owned a running store called the Running Phoenix and sold running shoes, shorts, shirts, and other accessories. I had this cool logo of a cherry red phoenix wearing blue shoes with a black stripe." To my surprise, I could not continue.

"What's a running store?"

"A running store is a…" The definition escaped me. "A running store is a… It's for people who enjoy running."

"And you can make money at it?" She gave a stare that said, 'Get a real job.' "I've been so lucky to feel the cool air of a spring morning or the hard driving fall rain." She gave me a 'dollar sign' gesture, as she ran her hand down her chest, *daddy's money*. My friend Lina told me what it meant when I received it from the landscapers in their neon green shirts. Memories of sweating the monthly payments filled me with resentment, but I did not confront her. *Don't try me. I lived on borrowed money, just like you.*

"Oh, come on – didn't you like track and field?" I asked.

Josephine gave a frosty reply. "I didn't have time for diversions." Tourner interrupted her, spinning round and round.

"Tourner se remettre au travail."

Tourner returned to searching.

"You've been watching Tourner. Do you like animals?" she asked.

"Yes, I had a cute tabby named Wheels." Worry confronted me as he needed to be fed. "I've got to go," I exclaimed. Josephine took a deep breath and looked at me curiously.

"Where are you going?"

"I must go." But I didn't move.

"I'm not stopping you," she said. I froze for another moment and left. I passed a bicyclist wearing red and blue shorts as I moved down an unfamiliar street, but I was familiar with this part of Chandler and Phoenix. Josephine said I had a new body. What could it do? A car passed by on a cross street and I pursued it. I sped up, reached the cross street and banked left like an airplane. The car was ahead and my body felt like an arrow, no a bullet, no a superhero. I overtook it, looked right, and saw the driver who was texting. "Hang up and drive," I yelled, not caring he could not hear me as I passed. Moving west, I reached Interstate ten, passing cars and trucks and feeling my superpowers. An exit sign for Ray Road reminded me what I had to do. I moved above the cars on the exit ramp and rose over the bridge. From there, I found my house. It looked like a museum, with the dust slowly accumulating. Gray carpet covered the living room floor and a flat screen television perched on a stand. The cable box sat next to and just behind the television. Wheels sat alone with his striped paws folded beneath him. I entered the kitchen and found his food dish empty. My hand passed through the handle of the refrigerator when I tried to open it. I passed through the metal door and entered. The cat food sat on the shelf, but my hand could not grasp it. Time passed and Wheels' suffering increased as he searched for food, but the house was too clean. "Wheels, I'm here." But he did not hear me as he meowed with a high whine.

I tried again to feed him, but to no effect.

"Maaaaaawwwwrrrr!" He laid down in a sphinx position.

"Someone feed my cat! Help him!" I had only two choices: Leave him or stay and watch him suffer. My superpowers evaporated as I stayed and wept.

"Wheels, I know you can't hear me but I'll stay with you. I love you so much."

"Maaaaaaaawwrrrrrr!"

My heartache increased with his suffering. Josephine and *Tourner* reappeared.

"You were hard to find. What do we have here?" she said.

"Mawwwwwrrrrrr!"

Tourner meowed and his question mark tail became rigid upon seeing Wheels. "Oh, poor kitty, he's so hungry," she said as she ran her hand down Tourner's back.

"Josephine, do something," I pleaded.

She looked at me with sympathetic eyes. "Dawn, I can bring

the entire animal kingdom here and it'll have no effect. Your cat is in the earthly life and we're in the eternal life."

"What can I do about his suffering?" I knew the answer as soon as the question left my lips.

"Dawn, as I said before, you're trying to apply the physical world of the earthly life to the eternal life."

The truth of her statement drained my strength. "I can't even feed a starving cat."

"Sad, but true." Despair flattened me.

"What good is eternal life if I can't even relieve this curable suffering? Better to die and fade to nothing." "Mawwrrrrrrrr!" Tourner meowed back and his glow reddened. "Silencieux," Josephine said to him. "He has a hard time seeing others suffer."

"Duh, I'm not having a tranquil time with this either." My light changed to a vicious red.

"Dawn, the only thing I can say is he won't suffer in the eternal life."

"Why should he suffer? I'm sorry Wheels for getting killed and letting you down." Guilt and shame stained me.

"Your death was an accident."

"Why does he have to suffer? I know! I know! We're in the eternal life!"

Josephine was silent as I wept shiny white tears. After I stopped, she replied.

"I know people who might have answers. Do you want to meet them?" Before I could answer, the front door unlocked, and my parents entered. Wheels ran toward them and I felt myself die all over again. "Maaaaawwwrrrr!"

"Oh, Wheels, I'm glad to see you too," said Mom as she held him in her arms. "Walter, check if he has food." Dad turned into the kitchen.

"No, it's been awhile." He opened the refrigerator door and took out the cat food. Wheels jumped out of Mom's arms, ran toward Dad and began purring loudly. Dad placed the cat food in the dish and Wheels quickly started eating, making 'smack smack' sounds.

"We must take him home," Mom said. She opened a closet door and pulled out a cat carrier.

"They're disposing my life." My voice cracked. "They're disposing your earthly life, which happens to all of us," Josephine said. "You need to understand you have a second chance." I wanted my first chance back, but remained silent. My parents put Wheels into the cat carrier after he finished eating and Tourner calmed down.

"We'll come back for the rest," Dad said. They left the house with Wheels, the lock turning with a click, leaving me alone.

"Looks like they'll take care of your cat." Her light looked like a soft blue and green flame. I should have felt relief instead of defeat.

Pointing at Tourner, I asked, "Why should animals suffer?" Resignation pinned me down as my light changed to a dull gray color.

"Why should anyone suffer? I said this before. There are people who can help you. Do you want to meet them?" She waited for me to respond and put her hands on hips. My vicious red light returned, which gave me a wave of pleasure.

"Yeah, they have some explaining to do." Josephine smiled. "OK, we'll go after I finish working here." We left my house, which would soon go to someone else. Twilight came and brought soft light, which bathed everything in soft colors. A photographer friend, who I had not seen in two years, called it the golden hour. We moved down the street as Tourner continued searching. "So what's your granny's name?" Josephine kept on moving. Her question caught me off guard.

"What?"

"What's your granny's name?"

"Anna Belle."

"Anna Belle, who?" She didn't look at me.

"Thorson, why?"

Tourner meowed repeatedly and gave off an agitated tint in red shades. "He found someone," Josephine said coolly.

"Indique-nous le chemin." Tourner led us to a house which looked identical to the others on the street. We passed through a wall and entered a bedroom. What I witnessed shocked me.

"Good God!" Josephine said, "He splintered his light!"

CHAPTER 2

Blood and gore peppered the lampshade and nightstand in mixed colors of red, white, pink, and yellow. A huge reddish-brown spot stained the bed and a gaseous stench filled the bedroom. A woman with blood-stained clothes and a face of broken glass cradled a face torn body. She screamed in a pitch I hoped I would never hear again.

"Hal, why couldn't we talk about it?" A teenage boy emitting a flashing splintered black light tried to get back into his body just the way I tried to get back into mine. He cried tears of fragmented light, which fell away and vanished. "Mom, it's not your fault. I'm sorry."

Josephine floated quietly while I screamed.

Hal froze when he saw us. He turned and redoubled his efforts to return to his body. "Mom!" he shrieked, but the woman continued to weep. Shade covered his midsection.

Josephine turned my way long enough to glare at me and then watched Hal. Meanwhile, the woman left the room and returned with a cell phone.

"911, what is your emergency?" A disembodied voice asked. It sounded more like a statement than a question.

I let out a moan and my light flashed black as the dialog between the woman and the 911 operator continued. Josephine turned again, but this time she got in my face.

"Get a grip!" She moved away and waited while I, stunned by her rebuke, just floated there. Hal stopped, turned to her and asked if she could help to get him back.

"That's not possible," Josephine said.

"But I need a second chance." Hal's light flashed so fast it looked steady. We watched him try to get back in his body, but I knew it would not happen.

"You'll have a second chance, but not in the earthly life," Josephine said in a chilled voice.

"Please!" he pleaded. The tears streamed off his face and vanished.

"I can't send you back. I'm only a woman," Josephine replied. Hal's begging eyes then looked at me.

"Me too," I said.

"Oh God, I should have left a note," he exclaimed.

Gasping sobs wracked his mother's breaths and a cry of agony came out of her twisted mouth. The sight of sudden death paralyzed her eyes open, revealing two black circles. A whiff of gunpowder directed my attention to the gun laying on the bed and the soaked blood touching its trigger safety.

"I don't think that would've helped." Josephine's face had the hard look of a police officer making an arrest.

"But I need to make it right." Hal looked like a trapped animal, who caught sight of the hunter.

Josephine put her hard face in Hal's eyes. "That'll have to wait until she passes through."

"Passes through?" His face looked blank.

"It's what you just did, but from your mother's point of view, you passed away," she said.

He pointed to his mother and pleaded. "Send me back for her sake."

Josephine's face would not yield. "You're not part of that life any more."

Hal's light continued flashing as he tried to bargain. "But I need to go back."

Josephine's voice clipped Hal's plea. "There's nothing I can do."

Seeing Hal plead for his life was like watching a drowning man. His arms flailed and his silhouette twisted and jerked, but the current pushed him to sea. A bird made from Lego blocks hung from the ceiling.

Three thin grey wires supported it and blue blocks made the body. Black blocks with yellow in the middle made the wings. Red and yellow blocks made the crown. The blocks were rectangular yet the bird showed graceful curves giving it the illusion of flight. It seemed like it flew in the age of the dinosaurs.

"The only thing you can do is to wait for your mother to come to this life," Josephine said.

"How long will that take?" Hal asked in resignation.

"It may be years." The woman set the cell phone down and cradled Hal's body. They were just a few feet away, but Hal's decision put them oceans apart. I gasped. Josephine did not glance back at me, but a brief streak of red flickered for a moment.

"Years?" his voice trailed off in despair and his flashing light changed to a dull splintered gray. His light flared yellow as he tried to make a deal. "Is it possible I can go back as a ghost and tell her I'm okay?"

"It doesn't work that way."

"There's got to be a way. They say ghosts exist." The gray hue pushed out the yellow.

Josephine's face refused to yield. "They don't."

Hal saw his light and screamed, changing it to black.

"What happened to me?"

"That light is a part of you, but you splintered it when you killed yourself. It's flashing black because you're scared and going through a change." She stopped speaking, moved closer, gave a soft smile and asked in a gentle voice, "Do you want a second chance?"

Hal shook his head. "Yes."

She touched him, forcing Hal to look her in the face.

"You only get one. So make the most of it." Hal nodded again. She carefully spoke her next words. "We can't make things right with your mother right now, but you can live a new life, which you can show her when she comes."

"Are you an angel?" he asked.

"Like I said, I'm a woman just in a different form."

"It's just as well you're not an angel. I don't deserve heaven." His pulsing abated and a steady glow took form. Josephine touched his hand.

"Sometimes we make the wrong decisions."

Sometimes we make the wrong decisions? He killed himself.

"You said my mother will come here?"

"Eventually, she will," Josephine replied.

"But you said that could take…" His voice trailed off.

"Yes, it may be a long time before she begins her eternal life."

"The what?"

"The eternal life," I said. "It's what we enter after we die in the previous life." A flicker of red passed through Josephine.

"Hal, this is Dawn, who also passed through today."

"Hi Dawn," Hal said.

"Hi," I said.

"Dawn got struck by lightning," Josephine declared.

"It must have been quite a shock," he said. The memory of

the scalpel shook me. Hal's face went blank while Josephine chuckled. "What's so funny?" Hal asked.

"Lightning – quite a shock." Josephine finished chuckling.

"Oh, I get it, sorry." His hue resembled an electrical short as I tried to forget the scalpel. Red and blue flashing lights of a police car appeared, spotlighting Tourner, who was sniffing a piece of Hal's body. The gore and the stench in the room made me queasy, changing my hue to disgusting shades of multiple colors.

"Uh-oh, looks like we should leave," Josephine said. "Dawn's changing colors." Tourner meowed. Hal looked at me, then away. We left the bedroom and saw the police car through the living room window. The flashing lights went off and two police officers approached the house. The porch light came on, but the darkness squeezed the light against the wall and the glow from the ceiling lamp stayed glued to the ceiling. Josephine turned to me, smiled and said we should leave before I become a Christmas tree. Hal said nothing, and I felt a burning red. *No way are you going to use me as a punch line for your eternal life.* Daddy's money. The words burned in my head. Josephine acted as if she did not notice, her blue and green light remaining unchanged. We left the living room. The doorbell rang and Josephine stopped. We passed through the open door when the woman answered it for the police officers. I wondered why we waited and then understood: Hal did not yet realize we could go through walls.

"Where are we headed and why am I floating?" Hal asked.

"Is there a park or school nearby?" Josephine asked.

"There's a school," he said.

"Can you show me the way?" Josephine asked.

"Why am I floating?" His light remained steady, but I could

sense the worry in his voice.

"It's part of the transition, nothing to worry about," Josephine said.

"How do I move?"

"Just follow me." We left the house through the open door, with Tourner bringing up the rear.

It was a standard red brick high school. I did not look for the name. A fence of vertical metal bars surrounded the school, making it appear like a prison instead of education. A surprised look crossed Hal's face as he passed through the bars. Josephine stopped us at a baseball field and pointed to the outlines of some bushes on the other side of the right field fence. "We'll stop there for the night," she said. We proceeded to the bushes and waited in the dark.

"What's next?" Hal asked.

Josephine let out a wide smile. "Let me tell you about my organization, The Society of Searchers."

A muddled look crossed Hal's face. "Who are they?"

Josephine's voice became louder. "The Society of Searchers is an organization of volunteers who search for the recently passed through and help them adjust to the eternal life. We go everywhere, from the streets of New York to the Amazon rain forest. We search for them all, the rich, the poor, the young, the old, the strong, and the weak and give them a second chance, if they want to take it."

"You go all over the world?" His light was bouncing.

"Yes, I do." Her blue and green tint brightened. "I've been to Italy, Morocco, France, Argentina, Chile, and many more places. Do you want to hear more?"

Hal's face changed from muddled to awe. "Yeah."

Double doors confined the light within a hallway, and the

glow from a nearby streetlight felt the weight of the dark. Everything else, the night covered in formless black. Hideous visions of the paintings of Hell by Bosch, Goya, and Bruegel the Elder from my college Art History class threatened to hijack my thoughts. Her blue and green hue bubbled as she told her tales about the places she had been and the people she had seen. At last, she stopped and asked Hal a question.

"Tomorrow, I'm going to join my fellow society members at a place called Hell Canyon, which is west of a town called Perkinsville, Arizona. Do you want to meet them?"

"Yes, I would," Hal said enthusiastically.

Josephine's gestures did not show if she was good or evil as my parents' warning about strangers blared in head and my silhouette's glow changed to black. I observed her body language, as I asked her a series of questions that I hoped would reveal her true colors.

"Where is Perkinsville, Arizona?"

Josephine's looked at me as an afterthought as her blue and green hue became still. "It's on the Verde River."

"I know where the Verde River is," Hal exclaimed. His splintered light also sparked blue and green.

I stifled the urge to tell him to shut up as I asked the next question. "Where is Hell Canyon?" The word 'Hell' made my silhouette twitch.

Josephine's face was immobile. "It's west of Perkinsville."

Hal said nothing as I asked a tougher question.

"What happens when we get to Hell Canyon?"

Josephine's reply had a neutral tone as Hal became more attentive. "You and Hal will go through orientation, which is the first step in helping you adjust to your new lives. Then you will meet people from other societies and you can decide whether to join them."

She listed some societies: Botanists, chemists, government, philosophy, foreign languages, and history.

"Do they have paleontology?" Hal asked.

"What's that?" Josephine asked.

"Dinosaurs," I said.

The flicker of red passed through Josephine as she said to Hal, "Yes, they do and they're real dinosaurs." Then she stopped and said to me with her eyes, 'Take your next shot'.

"So when do we go?" Hal's splintered light was bouncing.

Josephine kept her eyes fixed on me. "Tomorrow, but you don't have to go."

"Oh, I'm going," Hal said.

I kept my eyes fixed on her and said, "Tomorrow it is."

But I knew she saw my black light.

Tourner cuddled against Josephine, and Hal's blue and green glow changed to black. He looked like a man serving the first day of a lengthy prison sentence as the enthusiasm he had earlier vanished. I peered into the night and thought about Tom and Summerhaven.

We were leaving the trailhead for Passage twelve of the Arizona Trail. A wave of lust mixed with a hint of fear washed through me. Fear he would use me. Fear he would break and reject me. The breakfast I just ate at a nearby restaurant called The Sawmill Run warmed me. Memories of the blue and white sign coming into town, saying 'Welcome to Summerhaven' and the smell of pine played with me. A memory of his statement jolted me.

"The wilderness begins in one mile. You'll see what Coronado saw back in 1540." Now I found myself in a wilderness without a trailhead. Panic rose as the darkness touched me.

Josephine's blue and green glow revealed nothing. In fact, she looked tranquil.

I peered into the night, wondering if she had accomplices, who would have many opportunities to attack. They could attack now straight out of the darkness, or on the Verde River, or wait for us at Hell Canyon. Hal's confused and scared silhouette now gave a brown and black glow.

A noise from behind, I whipped my head but saw nothing. I prepared for an attack but nothing happened and Josephine's glow did not change, nor did she move. She said the lights reveal my emotions and my silhouette emitted a deep black light. I had to change the color to show her I was in control.

Josephine's hue gave her an appearance of confidence and serenity. I willed myself to be just as calm and collected, but my colors stayed the same. Out of nowhere, Dad's advice emerged.

Control your fear.

A blue and green light emerged and partially pushed out the black as I attempted to do so. I fought harder as I recalled the tight spot I was in with my business on the Fourth of July, but my light remained at blue, green, and black despite my attempts. I saw Josephine and remembered that smile when she said 'Christmas tree' and 'daddy's money'. *I will not be your punch line.* My red flared, pushing the blue and green forward while evicting the black. A flush of victory bathed me as I admired the tint, but I became dismayed when I compared it to Josephine's hue. My blue and green appeared strained and pale with hints of black while hers was dark and burned pure like prized sapphire and emerald.

My black rushed back as another noise came out of the dark.

***

The grass slowly turned green and to my relief, the sky's eastern darkness showed a faint blue. "The first night's the toughest," Josephine said. *She could have got me, and she can still get me.* Hal was staring at the ground. The daylight strengthened and gave colors and definition to my surroundings. Joy flowered within me and a blue and green glow pushed away the black upon seeing the right field grass and the sharp-cornered walls of the high school. Hal jolted as Josephine caught his attention. "How's my man holding up?" Josephine asked. For an instant, his face revealed a pink tint.

"Uh, fine."

"Are you blushing?" Josephine chuckled. The pink tint charged back in a darker shade as Hal covered his face. "Hal, you have rosy cheeks. Is it because I referred to you as a man?" Her eyes twinkled.

"I'm not blushing," Hal repeated.

"Why are you covering your face?" Josephine teased.

"Come on, show me what you look like pink." Hal kept his face covered.

"No."

Josephine kept coaxing. "Come on. Come on. It's okay. Blushing only means you're honest." Hal lowered his hands, revealing a hot pink face. Josephine touched him as if he was of the finest porcelain. The lights in the double doors winked off. "Was it because I referred to you as a man?"

"Yes," Hal stammered.

"Really, I thought girls called you that all the time," she said.

"You're the first woman who called me a man." His words sounded like a shameful confession.

"We need to open their eyes," she said.

"You can do that?" His eyes widened as if she had the keys to manhood.

"Yes, I can. Now are you ready to go to Hell Canyon?"

She's using him! A flash of guilt reminded me what Becky and I did to a boy named Kyle. Hal's face shone as if expecting to find gold, and I sensed him slipping into Josephine's orbit, whose smile revealed nothing. He didn't get that we knew as much about her as runaways knew about strange cities.

Hal exuded confidence. "Yes, I am."

"Then let's go." She said it like a travel agent.

"What's in it for you, Josephine?" My voice was sharp and my silhouette twitched as the paintings of Bosch, Goya, and Bruegel the Elder danced in my head.

"I'm part of the Society of Searchers. It's what we do." She looked at my stare and said, "You don't believe me," in a flat voice.

"Everything has a price," I said in a hard tone.

"This is the eternal life. No matter what you think I want, I can get." She pointed to Tourner and asked, "*Souhaitez-vous que vos amis vous rejoignent?*"

"Mawr!"

She opened up her arms with a showman's air and exclaimed, "*Venir mes enfants!*" Out of nowhere, all these animals appeared in silhouette and the noise they made sounded like the animal kingdom version of rush hour. Some I recognized like the dogs, cats, and horses, but others had an appearance all their own. A cheetah came up to Josephine and sat next to her. "Come here, Chiquita. Yes, you are pretty today."

"You have a cheetah named Chiquita?" I had to shout over the noise.

"Yes, we were fond of each other and we reunited after I

passed through." She stroked his chin. "He waited for me."

"You had a pet cheetah in the earthly life?" I asked skeptically.

"Yes, I did. I had to feed him a steady diet of pigeons, but the eternal life has one advantage. I can have all the animals I want and I don't have to worry about feeding or cleaning up after them." I stared in amazement as the colossal piece of the animal kingdom floated next to her, hanging around as if they were on jury duty. One of them had oversized fangs but before I could say anything, Hal shouted with that typical little boy amazement.

"Is that a sabercat?"

"What?" Josephine responded.

"Is that a sabercat?" The noise intensified.

"What?" Hal waved his hands, and Josephine quieted the animals with one word.

"Silencieux!" she shouted. Instantly, the animals were quiet. "Yes, that's a sabercat. His name is Stan," she said.

"The eternal life has extinct animals?" I asked.

"The eternal life has all creation," she replied.

"Wow, a camelops!" Hal exclaimed. He pointed to an animal that looked like a pony-sized camel.

"A what?" I asked.

"A camelops!" he said. "And a glyptodon!" He pointed to another animal that looked like it had an oversized turtle shell.

"So that's what they're called," Josephine said.

"Why are they not fighting each other?" I asked.

"Because the eternal life is not a fight for survival," Josephine replied. She gazed at an animal that looked like a deer. "I haven't seen him before." I noticed I did not have hunger or thirst. I looked back at the animals.

"They're so exotic," I said.

"Yes, they are, and beautiful, too." A smile leaked out of her. "If we're going on a trip, then let's bring friends," Josephine said. She looked Hal in the eye and said, "I need a *man* to lead us to the Verde River. Can you do that for me?" Her eyelashes fluttered.

"Yeah, yes Josephine, I can do it." Hal's tongue stuttered. *I need a man to lead us to the Verde River. What a user.* I imitated her fluttering eyelashes.

"Once we reach the Verde River, we must find Hell Canyon," Josephine continued.

"I know where the Verde River is. You can count on me." *You can count on me.* I suppressed my disgust.

"Thanks, Hal. You're a marvelous man." Hal's face gave off a blue and green glow. The sun continued its ascent as we left the high school. I glanced back at the brown shade of the pitcher's mound and the green hue of the infield grass. We continued over a street. My parent's warnings about strangers dried my mouth. I tried to stall one last time.

"We can't go!" I said.

"What do you mean we can't go?" Josephine's light flickered red and brown before returning to blue and green. My bruised light flashed, which betrayed my thoughts.

"I need to say goodbye to my parents."

"Dawn, you'll do that at your funeral, which we'll tell you about at Hell Canyon. You'll need to say goodbye to everyone."

Her omission about the funeral fueled my suspicions as red and black light illuminated my silhouette.

"You didn't mention this last night."

Hal's silhouette twitched for an instant.

Josephine's color held firm. "You'll see them at your funeral, which will come soon enough, but this is more important."

My color changed to a wounded purple. "I'm seeing my parents!"

"You can go see your parents, but we will not wait for you." Her hue blinked yellow for a moment as she pivoted and asked Hal in an urgent voice, which sounded like an order. "Are you going to follow me?"

Hal's light changed to black, and his face tightened. "Yes."

Anxiety welled up as they moved away. Once they left, I would be alone and Josephine was my only protection, although she was potentially dangerous. I joined them.

"Okay, we'll do it your way."

Josephine didn't reply.

Hal led us to State Route 202 and from there, we headed east at a slow pace until we reached the Beeline Highway, where we headed north as if going to Payson. Most of the animals with us had drifted off, but Tourner, Chiquita, and Stan stayed with us along with a few dogs. Hal enjoyed watching the traffic stream below, the cars and trucks looking like multicolored fish. We moved over a sign that said 'Entering Salt River Pima Maricopa Indian Reservation'. "It should be the next bridge after we pass the Fort McDowell casino," he said.

"Thank you, my man," Josephine replied. Hal's glow flickered pink for a moment. Then a shadow passed over us. The silhouette of a gigantic bird resembling the mobile in the bedroom, circled in the air, giving off a soft gray hue. As it descended, it looked like a lizard. Its profile revealed a large crested head of red and yellow and its wings looking like they were of leather.

"Is that a flying lizard?" I asked. It resembled the model hanging in Hal's bedroom.

"What are you talking about?" Josephine asked.

"Wow, cool!" Hal exclaimed. Josephine saw what we were seeing.

"Yes, they fly around often," she replied. "You see one dinosaur you've seen them all."

"That's a pterosaur," Hal said.

"Pterosaur, dinosaur – what's the difference?" Josephine muttered.

"They have different evolutionary histories," Hal said.

"Where did you learn this?" I asked.

"I visited the Smithsonian when Mom took me to Washington D. C." His voice trailed off after Mom. Josephine gave me a look.

We passed another sign saying 'Entering the Fort McDowell Indian Reservation'. Right after that, we saw a casino video screen inviting us to play. We went by the casino and stopped at a bridge, which had a sign in white lettering and green background that said Verde River. There were the green trees I could only glance at when driving to Payson. Dust blew over the highway and up the river. I remembered the Ash Wednesday saying. From dust you came to dust you return. "We're just like the dust." my words sounded unusually loud.

"Not quite," Josephine replied. "The wind moves the dust. We, however, can decide where to go." The dust crossed the river and dissipated in the desert air.

Hal interrupted us. "I want to go home."

"But I need a *man* to show me the way," Josephine said.

"Hal, we can't return, but we don't have to be alone," I replied. Josephine shot me a short quick glare followed by a red flash. Hal just stared at me. "Hear me out, Hal, please," I said. "We both want to go back, but we know we can't." I recalled Josephine's offer. "Josephine is promising you a second chance.

Make her deliver." The red glare on her face showed me I crossed her. *Come and get me. Come and get a bellyful of daddy's money.*

"Hal, why don't you check out that – camelops? I must talk to Dawn," Josephine said.

"OK." Hal went away.

"You're a real piece of work!" she said. She let red colors fly. I did the same.

"Look who's talking. I need a *man* to show me the way?"

"And you think you know what you're doing?"

"Hey, I was just trying to help you out. You were floundering."

"I've come for the dying alcoholics, murdered prostitutes, rich bankers, and now the vanilla girl of Phoenix." Her hands clenched. "Don't disrespect me."

"You can't handle vanilla!"

"I've been around the world in the earthly and eternal lives. I can handle any flavor, and yours is plain."

"Your mind has a rich fantasy life." We stared into each other's eyes as our colors burned hotter. As we stared, I noticed I did not feel the need to blink.

"OK, I'm back." Hal's face brightened. "That animal is amazing. Oh sorry, do you still need time?"

"No, we're done," Josephine replied. "Thanks for giving us the time and I'm glad you like the animal." She softened her voice, expanded her chest, and said, "I still a need a *man* to lead me to Hell Canyon. Will you help me?"

Hal's face lit up and his voice cracked. "Will do!" He tried again, but this time with a deep sound. "I mean, will do."

"Take us to Hell Canyon," Josephine said. Hal's face had a blank look, reminding me of my first date. *He doesn't know the way.* "Hal, why are you waiting? What's wrong?" Her voice rose slightly. *She has no clue other than it's west of Perkinsville.* I suppressed a snort.

"I'm all right," Hal said. "It's just… Never mind."

"I understand," she replied. His voice cracked again.

"This way." Again, he deepened his voice. "I mean, this way." That also happened on my first date. We went upstream, and I enjoyed myself. *Fake it 'til you make it. Hal, you're such a guy.* The water's monotone sound and moist smell was soothing, and the green trees and bushes hugging the water provided a beautiful contrast to the harsh tans of the stone and sand. The horizon showed a distant mountain. I would never have seen this part of the river in my earthly life or park the car at the bridge to explore it. My silhouette twitched again.

"Worried I'm taking you to Hell, Vanilla?" Josephine said.

"Ha. Ha."

"You're acting like you have crickets in your panties."

Hal's mouth dropped open.

Daddy's money. I gritted my teeth. "I'm just fine. Plenty of places called Hell."

"Some of them really are."

We continued upriver. Chiquita and Stan stopped to watch some deer lingering a bit before catching back up to us.

"So, what else happens at Hell Canyon?" I kept my silhouette rigid.

"You'll find out," she replied curtly. She had the knowledge, which meant she had the power, which I had to get. I tried to start a conversation.

"So how did you become the name?"

"It was because of my dancing and singing."

"Really?"

"I had the grace and the moves to pull it off, unlike most

girls. They shook their hips as if they were trying to get the last bit of catsup out of an already empty bottle."

"So you were a dancer?"

"You can say that." She said it as if giving me permission to be correct.

"What did you sing?"

She went silent. I kept asking questions, but to no avail. "I take it you don't want to talk any more."

"You're learning."

Hal, however, had not. "Hey, Josephine, why are all these animals attracted to you?" Hal asked.

"It took a lot of time, but once they realized I cared, it was easy." *Maybe Hal could help me.* I waited, hoping he could open her up.

"Do they do tricks like sit up and roll over?"

"*Stan, viens ici,*" Josephine commanded. Stan went over. He had a tan silhouette, glittering oversized teeth, and a jet-black nose. His muzzle was short and broad and with ears pinned next to his head. A mane flowed off his back, and his muscles revealed the torso and legs that made him a force in the earthly world. "What would you like him to do?" Josephine asked.

"I don't know—roll over?" Hal said.

"*Rouler.*" The sabercat rolled over. She rubbed his belly. "*S'asseoir.*" Stan sat up and then purred as Josephine rubbed his belly again. "*Un tel magnifique kitty.*" She rubbed his ear. "*Mendier.*" Stan begged and received another belly rub.

"Josephine, you're magic!" Hal exclaimed.

"Thank you, Hal. Many men have said I was magic, but from you it rings true. Do you get what I mean?" Hal looked like he was about to pay a stiff price.

"Ah, er, ummmm, no."

"It's because you mean what you say. Women like that." Hal beamed, and I rolled my eyes. He was a normal, never-been-kissed fifteen-year-old boy who did not understand that he was a masculine pigeon to this feminine cheetah. The shade around his groin lightened. *Oh God, he likes her.* I looked at Stan and sighed. The once mighty hunter now an oversized domesticated tabby. *Why can't you take a nice oversized bite out of her?* The picture of his fangs puncturing Josephine gave me pleasure.

"Are we going to continue moving upriver or are we going to do stupid pet tricks?" I said.

"My, don't we have an attitude?" she said.

"She was only doing something nice," Hal said.

"Sorry Hal, you're right. It was nice." I said. "She's the kind you can take home to mother."

I regretted the words immediately. Hal's splintered light darkened and gave off a wounded purple glow. I just floated there, feeling my colors turn pink while he said nothing. "Hal, I'm sorry. I didn't mean to hurt you," I said.

"You just had to hurt him," Josephine said.

"I didn't mean to hurt him. I just said something dumb without thinking." Josephine poured it on.

"Do you think at all?" She turned to Hal.

"Why don't you join me and the animals?"

"God, I miss her so much. The pain, does it ever stop?"

"Hal, I'm sorry," I repeated.

"Shut up!" His stinging rebuke taught me words are as powerful in the eternal life as the earthly life.

"Let's keep going," Josephine said. I wanted to turn back as I wondered how long the implications of my words would last as we continued upstream. We passed several towns. A sign for one said Clarkdale. Stan, Chiquita, and Tourner led the way. A mournful train whistle parted the air and faded away as I glanced at some rocks in the water. "Are you sure we're on the Verde River?" Josephine asked Hal. Her voice rose slightly, which made me smile. Hal tried to make his voice sound deep.

"That's what the sign said." I felt the pleasure of her discomfort as her face betrayed a slight strain.

"Where is it?" She muttered.

"We're going to run out of light soon," Hal said. His face betrayed worry and confusion. The trees and bushes on the riverbanks seemed to hide everything. A squirrel skittered up a tree. Soon the trees and bushes gave way to rocks and scrub, and the riverbanks got higher and steeper. Twilight approached and my stomach tightened some more. I no longer found the confused look he had at the bridge funny. We entered a canyon, and the air darkened.

"This should be Hell Canyon," Josephine said. Her voice hit higher notes and her glow showed a hint of black. Hal didn't seem to hear her as his face changed to a desperate gambler.

"Are you sure?"

"Of course, I'm sure."

You're so fake.

"Welcome to Hell Canyon, ladies," a male voice said, as he stepped out of a tree. His silhouette showed he had a face so square his cheekbones looked like sharp corners, and an aura of neutral colors suppressing a red hue.

"Dammit, Mitch, I hate it when you use the chameleon light," Josephine said. Mitch gave Josephine a deadpan look.

"I thought you liked surprises. Don't tell me it's over between us."

Josephine just looked at him, which Mitch took as his cue to deliver another punch line.

"Where are your manners, Josephine? Aren't you going to introduce me to your friends?"

"Mitch, meet Hal and Dawn."

"Good evening, welcome to Hell Canyon and your second chance," he said.

I sensed Mitch was angry.

Chapter 3

My silhouette twitched as the remaining light in Hell Canyon vanished, leaving behind a cave-like darkness that even concealed the nearby trees. Only the sounds of crickets and the river current showed anything was out there.

"Do you think that's cool?" Mitch asked Hal.

Hal's splintered light brightened. "Yeah, can you show me how?"

"I'll show you tomorrow morning, when we can see what we're doing, right after orientation."

The businesswoman in me intervened as I gave him a hard stare, holding it long enough to make sure he knew not to mess with me.

"What's your price?"

Mitch gave an amiable smile. "Cost exists only in the earthly life."

I kept the stare. "Everything has a price."

His smile remained unchanged, and Mitch must have observed my body language.

"In the earthly life, that's true. In the eternal life, it's not. I had your suspicions, too."

"So it's orientation tomorrow." I held my look and kept my voice measured and smooth as I mentally confirmed Josephine's earlier statement.

Josephine sneered. "Tonight, we'll give you time for yourself and then tomorrow you'll meet the group and learn more about your second chance." Mitch's grin didn't flinch.

"The group?" I asked.

"You two aren't the only ones who passed through," Josephine said.

"Are you a Searcher like Josephine?" Hal asked. Josephine's blue and green hue became more vivid in the dark, while Mitch's changed to a light blue and green.

"Yes, I am and you'll learn more about us at orientation, but we, for now, must leave," he said.

"See you both at sunrise," Josephine said.

"You plan to wake us up?" I asked.

"You no longer need sleep," she said. Mitch and Josephine left us in the dark before I could ask any more questions. As they left, I heard Mitch say, "We need to talk." I didn't hear her response. Hal's face tightened and his hue changed to a flashing black.

"I'm going to Hell."

His words chilled my back. "Why do you think you're going to Hell?"

"Because of what I did. It's just a matter of time." His eyes had the look of something coming for him.

My hue flickered red for an instant as I glanced around in the darkness for Josephine and Mitch. *What were they thinking, leaving us alone?* "Who says you're going to Hell?"

"I killed myself."

"Mitch said there's an orientation. Let's see what he says."

Hal's eyes kept peering into the darkness and the fear in his face and his black hue urged me to do something, but I was just as lost. Words popped into my head, which I said without thinking.

"They're going to have to come through me first."

Hal gave me a hopeful look. "You'll protect me?"

An idea surfaced. "How about we protect each other?"

Hal's light stopped flashing. His black glow faded and his face filled with relief. "You can count on me." He moved next to me, and after a while, his hue changed to a neutral color. Unable to see anything and the silence of the black night made me squirm, so I asked him a question.

"That model hanging in your bedroom, was it a pterosaur?"

Hal grabbed my question. "Yes, it is. How did you know?"

The words spilled out of him like a waterfall. He told me about the Smithsonian and its mummies, dinosaurs, and extinct mammals. He spoke at length about the 'Fossilab', where they cut the fossils out of rocks, and described the Hope Diamond exhibit. His eyes danced when he described the diamond's steely blue color and its red glow. He spoke as if he never got the chance to talk. He told me about the time he met a paleontologist in Utah who showed him the tools he used to reveal the teeth, legs, claws, spikes, and horns of the fossils. At last, Hal's flood of words abated. "Thanks, Hal. I appreciate it, but let's be quiet for a bit." Much as I liked him, his words left me tired. I listened to the chirping of crickets and the river's flow. The canyon and its grim night gave me the feeling I was in a back alley, which intensified my worries. A breeze passed by and the smell of grass wafted past me. Thoughts of tomorrow circled me and I wished for sleep, if only to a hide for a while.

A woman's voice nearby startled us. "My work has been just fine," she said. A man's voice replied, saying something unintelligible. Curious, we investigated, and the voices became louder as we approached. We stopped at a bush and peered through its branches. There, in a clearing, Josephine and Mitch were arguing.

"Your work has been slipping for a long time, Josephine." His words sounded like a slapped face.

Josephine flinched but put her eyes back on Mitch. "My work has been just fine," she repeated.

"Not lately, you were ill-prepared for this assignment."

Hal and I looked at each other with open mouths as he continued.

"I got them here, didn't I?" Josephine's silhouette quivered for a fleeting moment before it firmed.

"I need a *man* to lead me to the Verde River." Mitch's words slapped her again, which I liked.

Josephine fidgeted and her silhouette went through several color changes before settling on an angry red. "You were spying on me?"

Mitch's glow flickered red for an instant. He raised his voice but maintained his composure. "I was monitoring your work, which is what supervisors *do,* and what I saw was unsatisfactory."

Mitch could have used the chameleon light to watch us at the high school.

"One of the fundamental rules of searching is knowing where to go once you find someone. You've been doing this since 1976. You know better."

Again, Josephine's silhouette went through multiple color changes. "I was just trying to get the kid to feel good about himself."

I glanced at Hal and saw the hurt in his face.

Mitch ignored her. "'Vanilla,' 'Do you think at all,' 'Are you sure we're on the Verde River?'"

Josephine's glow shifted to red, but it lost some of its luster. "I was just…"

Sensing that our lights stood out in the darkness, I motioned to Hal to follow me and watch from inside a branch.

"You were unprepared and unprofessional." The tone of Mitch's voice and the look in his eyes sliced off her words. Then his manner softened. "You're burning out, Josephine. Your fluency in Spanish, French, German, and Italian helped you reach people. There's your war service during the Iran-Iraq war, where you helped countless soldiers cope with their passing through even though you couldn't speak a lick of Farsi or Arabic. But now they look the same to you. It shows."

A hint of purple flickered through her silhouette. "Shut up!"

Mitch's voice remained unchanged and his silhouette took an aggressive stance. "For now, I will. One more thing, Virgil will come to help Hal."

"No, not him."

"I don't get you. He's a nice guy. Anyway, he's coming. I'll see you tomorrow and think about what I said." Mitch left.

A twinge of guilt passed through me as I recalled how Becky and I mistreated Kyle back in high school. Hal's light flashed. I touched him. "I said I'll protect you."

Hal didn't reply, but his light steadied. Then we froze as Josephine looked in our direction.

Her silhouette bled purple as she wept. "I'm the name. I'm the name," she repeated. *"Venir mes enfants,"* she called. Her animals quietly arrived and rubbed against her. She stroked the camelop's ear and asked it a question, which she answered. *"Suis-je le nom?"*

"Yes, I *am* the name." She did the same with Stan and Chiquita. Blue and green mingled with purple, and to our relief, she left.

Hal and I looked at each other. "What just happened?" I

asked.

I thought about Kyle and concluded Josephine and I had one thing in common. We mistreated men.

"I'm sorry, Mom," Hal said under his breath.

The cave-like darkness concealed our shame.

The eastern sky's darkness faded to reveal Hell Canyon's eroded walls. The minutes before sunrise presented a powder blue sky and pink-tinted clouds. A trail marker said Hell Point Trail #9012. A light green bird with a gray crest and grooved wings took flight. Another bird with a bright red crest preened itself and danced on the river's edge, and an orange-brown bird ran through the rock. Countless other birds chatted in thick-leafed trees. Josephine approached, accompanied by Tourner, whose question mark tail stood erect.

"Good Morning, Josephine," I said. "It's so beautiful today, as if we're in heaven. So strange this place is called Hell Canyon."

"Well, it's not a good morning and you're not in heaven." She replied.

I gave a mock salute. "Excuse me, Sergeant Josephine."

"That's *Lieutenant* Josephine, to you." She took a wide stance and gave me a look saying, "Cross that line again, *please.*"

Eager to avoid crossing that line, I kept my mouth shut.

"Follow me." She and Tourner led us downstream, where we met Mitch and the group.

"Welcome to orientation. Are you ready to make some new friends?" Mitch was as cheerful as Josephine was grumpy. People with black and brown lights and confused and worried expressions milled about and held conversations in groups of twos and threes. I counted and found there were forty-eight of them, including Hal and I. Some conversations were in English, others in Spanish, and still others in Chinese. The silhouettes of some had an ivory color like mine. Others had a deep coffee color, a smooth yellow color, or a color of a unique shade. Their hues had varying shades of brightness, and none of them had bruised or splintered lights. I wondered what their stories were. Another group of men and women with similar silhouettes were nearby, talking among themselves. They had neutral hues and relaxed facial expressions.

"I'll conduct the orientation class in English, but it is helpful to learn foreign languages," Mitch said to us. He then said to Hal, "Hey, we have a few minutes. Do you want to learn how to use your chameleon light?"

"Sure."

They proceeded to a green bush. "This is one color, so let's start with this." Mitch's hue changed to a green that was a shade darker than the bush. The green then flickered to a shade lighter and then matched the color. It was like matching paint colors at the hardware store. I barely saw his outline.

He could have been at the high school.

Hal's voice brightened. "Can I try?"

"Sure."

Hal's hue fluttered between bright and dark shades of green. He looked like splashed paint compared to Mitch's neat camouflage.

"Be patient and practice," Mitch said.

I pointed to the other group? "Who are they?"

"Other searchers," Mitch said.

Josephine was not among them.

"Good morning, everyone. Can we gather please?" he asked. The groups of twos and threes slowly merged. Once he confirmed he had their attention, he began. "Welcome to your first day and your second chance," he announced with a sunny voice. "My name is Mitch." There were some scattered, subdued good mornings in response. I wondered if he would say 'I can't hear you' or 'In this room I see a lot of potential' but thankfully he did not.

"I know you have gone through a major change in your life."

"Like duh, we just passed through," Someone muttered.

"Gets no more major than that," he retorted. The group released a tight laugh.

Mitch pointed to the other group. "Ladies, gentlemen, could you introduce yourselves?"

They responded sequentially. "Norma, Patricia, Joe, Mike, Sally."

"Now that we have the introductions out of the way, let's begin. I have much to tell you, starting with our organization, the Society of Searchers."

Mitch said the Society originated in several parts of the world to help the passed through adapt to the eternal life, but nobody knew how it began or how the separate societies merged. He explained the Society would help us adjust to our new forms, let go of our past, and begin our eternal lives. He said representatives from other societies such as the Order of the Veteran, the Chemist Club, and the Biology League, would come and visit. It felt like college sororities seeking pledges.

Mitch's words sounded too polished, probably because he said them many times before. I could picture his presentation in some nondescript hotel conference room. We would all sit in uncomfortable chairs drinking coffee from Styrofoam cups. "I'll help you adjust, but I will not sugarcoat it for you. It will be rough coping with the end of your earthly life and the beginning of your eternal life. However, you will learn the basics of the eternal life, which we will discuss in more detail later."

Mitch changed to a booming voice. He could have been wearing a gray suit preaching to a televised audience on Sunday morning. "You have a new body now, which is your silhouette, the source of your earthly and eternal lives. Do you want to know more?" Everybody nodded their heads. I half expected him to ask, "Do you want Jesus to save you?" A man translated Mitch's words into Spanish for a woman.

Mitch continued his infomercial. "Our parents created the silhouette during conception, which is too small for science to detect. A light emerges from the silhouette during pregnancy and both develop into an identity as mother and father nurture the baby. After birth, the light and silhouette strengthens as the parents raise the child."

A finger of sunlight peeked over the canyon and illuminated him as the booming voice thundered. His speaking style, though powerful, had a flaw. He never changed pitch, which gave his presentation a monotone hum as he described how the child intensifies the light and defines the silhouette during the earthly life by developing relationships. He summarized the relationships affecting light and silhouette: childhood, school, careers, government, religion, science, love, sex, marriage, and parenthood. I watched a tree branch float down the river when at last his tone changed, showing the infomercial was ending. "Then your body passed away, releasing your silhouette. *You* are at the beginning of your second chance. Do you understand?"

We all nodded. The man who was translating asked a question.

"How come the black holes don't have a light?"

I perked up. *What are the black holes?*

"Because they mixed in enough darkness to blot out their

light," Mitch explained. "We mix darkness with light when we abuse others. Now they must flee for eternity and will burn if caught." A pang of loneliness tightened my chest when another man asked how he could find his parents.

"Your life needs to take priority," Mitch said. The man's color and the colors of others flashed red for an instant. The next question was about me.

"Why does her light look bruised?" he asked. I could see all ninety-two eyes turn to me.

"That's because Dawn died an untimely death."

He looked at me and said the next words softly, as if asking me to tell how Jesus came into my life. "Would you tell them what happened?"

I wanted to say 'no' but said, "Lightning bolt, the feeling was electric." Everyone chuckled.

Mitch took back the floor. "People the cause of someone's death is very personal. We'll discuss it here because you need to know about these things, but generally we do not discuss it in public."

Another question and it was about Hal.

"Why does his light look splintered?"

Mitch's face tightened. "It's because he killed himself."

An awkward silence enveloped us. Hal looked like he was dying again. Mitch intervened. "Don't worry, Hal. You have a second chance." The silence returned. I wanted to know more about the black holes.

"Mitch, can you tell us more about the black holes?"

His face went serious and his voice took a dark tone.

"Yes, I can. The black holes are people condemned to hide from you or anything else emitting light. They resemble bedbugs and will burn if you catch them."

"Who are they?" a man in the group asked.

"They're the people who chose to be robbers in their earthly lives, the murderers who are the robbers of life, the rapists who are the robbers of sex, and the con men, swindlers, burglars, and arsonists, who are the robbers of labor."

"Are they in Hell?" A woman's voice asked.

Mitch gave her answer some thought and said, "To flee for eternity without hope of sanctuary, yeah, I suppose they are."

The glow from Hal's silhouette turned black and flashed. I held his hand.

"It's okay Hal, you have light," I whispered.

The flashing stopped, but he kept shaking.

"Let's take a few minutes before we continue," Mitch declared. Our group separated into clusters of twos and threes, while the size of the other group remained unchanged.

"Hey Hal, let's meet some people." I didn't check to see if he followed.

Nobody in the small groups would make eye contact, and Hal did not accompany me. Disappointed, I moved toward the group of searchers whose presence I found intimidating. I was close enough to hear a woman ask another woman, who had a bruised light, "When are we going back to NAU?"

Northern Arizona University, do we have something in common? I rushed to meet them.

"Excuse me. By any chance, did you go to NAU?"

They had ivory silhouettes that gave off a bubbly blue and yellow hue and greeted me as if I was an adorable kitten.

"Well hello, yes we did and who found you?" The one on the left asked.

"Josephine."

They exchanged glances. Their names were Norma and

Patricia. They were in the class of ninety-one while I was in the class of 2007. Norma majored in Economics and minored in Dance. Patricia majored in Economics and minored in English. It felt like a family reunion as we talked about our college days. We talked about everything NAU: bars, dorms, professors, and classes. Sensing I could trust them, I asked them a question about Josephine.

"I heard a rumor about Josephine and Virgil."

"That she doesn't like him. Everyone knows that." Patricia's bruised light sparkled.

"The story's juicier than that, Patricia," Norma said.

I looked back to see if Mitch was recalling us, but nothing showed orientation was about to resume. "Tell me."

"Here's the short version," Patricia said.

Patricia told me Virgil was a Knight of Malta who passed through during the Siege of Malta in 1564. He made many friends and had his share of women over the centuries, which included Italian women from the Renaissance and Russian women from the nineteenth century. I stopped her.

"Wait, he's been in the eternal life for four centuries?"

"You're a newbie, all right. Please let me continue."

I nodded.

She told me Virgil was in Paris when he and his friends went to the *Folies Bergere* Theater to watch a band from America perform a musical called *La Revue Negre*. According to the story, the theater went dark, and a spotlight appeared on center stage upon a palm tree where Josephine, who was wearing a two-piece costume, descended to the stage floor. The top piece, which seemed made of jewels, dubiously covered her breasts and the bottom piece comprised sixteen rubber bananas, which unsurely covered her hips and the tops of her thighs. At the thump of a bongo drum, she performed the *danse sauvage or* savage dance.

"What happened?"

"What do you think happened? He fell for her, except there was a slight problem."

"She was still living her earthly life," Norma said.

"Wow!" I exclaimed.

"There's more," Norma said. She said Virgil tried to court Josephine when she passed through, but the words came out wrong. He learned poetry and alternative forms of dance and offered them to her, but she has refused to listen to a single stanza or watch a single step to this day.

I couldn't believe she would pass up a man willing to learn dance and poetry for her. "Why doesn't she give him a chance?"

"We think she's afraid of men," Patricia said.

"She holds her shade pretty tightly," Norma said.

Patricia winked. "Makes it easier for us."

"We build up a man's heart only to destroy it utterly and completely," Norma said.

"Yuhhhht," they said in unison and laughed.

"How long has he been pursuing her?"

"Since 1976," they replied.

"His desire for her is legend," Patricia said.

I glanced back and did not see Mitch or Josephine. The silhouette of a strange bird flew overhead. *Where were all the dinosaurs?* Josephine said everything passes through to the eternal life. With all the animals, people, and plants that existed before us, the eternal life should look like a London train station. The canyon, however, showed just a sprinkling of glowing plants. *If everything comes to the eternal life, then why don't I see more of them?*

"Orientation should start up again," Patricia said.

The groups of twos and threes merged. I knew I needed to ask them more questions about Josephine before returning, but I gazed at Patricia's bruised light.

"You want to know how I got my bruise," Patricia said.

My color turned pink. "Sorry, I didn't mean to stare."

"It's okay. You newbies are just curious. I was driving to my job on the Indian reservation when a fully loaded hay truck squashed me and my car into a guardrail. It took the paramedics hours to cut me out. I guess God decided not to give me a 'bale' out, get it bale-out." She laughed.

I found it perplexing she found her untimely demise funny. "How can you laugh at your death?"

"First rule for your second chance, have a sense of humor."

I barely absorbed her words when she said, "Now Norma passed through, courtesy of a paper cut."

I looked at Norma, who looked at her hand. "Yeah, it got infected. The bacteria spread, and it was over in two weeks despite the doctors' best attempts."

"Wow," was all I could say.

"I need you all to gather again, please and learn about your second chance," Mitch announced.

Concerned I might not see them again, I asked them one last question. "Is there anything else I should know about Josephine?"

They glanced at each other. Patricia fixed her eyes on me. "She has a lot of French friends, so be careful what you do and say."

Why should I be careful of her French friends? I thanked them and was about to leave when Norma said, "One more thing, we didn't have this conversation."

What's so bad about this conversation? I found Hal and the group reconvened. Mitch continued the orientation while I wondered why I had to be careful.

"Look around you," he said.

Sunlight glinted off the cliffs. The birds were quiet.

"You stayed on streets in your earthly lives. A few of you may have been on trails, but you've seen so little of this world. Now's your chance to explore and do things you couldn't do."

Memories of Tom and the Arizona Trail returned. Oh, how I couldn't wait to see what was around the next corner. The sunlight's angle changed to reveal the cliffs' sharp lines.

"No need to worry about money or safety," he said.

The faces of the group revealed nothing. The business woman in me told me to wait for the price.

"As you know, I'm a member of the Society of Searchers here to help you adjust to your new lives. Over the next few weeks, you will meet people from other societies and clubs. You can leave with them or stay here. Now, I give you an important assignment."

Here it comes.

"You must attend your funeral, which marks the end of your earthly life and the beginning of your eternal life. Your searcher will tell you where it is and when it will take place."

Hal's face tightened. The thought of saying goodbye to everyone made my stomach churn.

"One of us can come with you. Seeing your coffin and watching people speak about you in the past tense can be hard to take."

A minister would officiate my funeral. Dad probably would wear his gray suit with red and blue tie, Mom a floral dress. Flowers would decorate my coffin. Who else would come? What would they say? *It's goodbye for good.* My breath became tight.

"How're they going to know where the funerals are?" a man in the group asked.

"We've been doing this for a while. Your searcher will give you the details," Mitch replied.

A silhouette joined the searchers as the orientation ended, followed by another silhouette with a question mark tail. It was Josephine, who looked like she was late for class, and Tourner. Orientation ended. Our group dispersed, and we returned to the ones who found us.

"Your funeral is tomorrow," Josephine said.

"But I only passed through…" Confusion set in. I lost my sense of time. "… two days ago."

"Funerals come fast," Josephine said. "Did you want them to marinate you, longer?"

Hal snickered. I gave him a look, and the snickering stopped.

"Where's it at and what time?" I think I asked.

I thought she said Desert Foothills Church, which made sense, as it was the church Mom and Dad attended.

"I think it was four-thirty," Josephine replied.

I snapped back to normal. "What do you mean you *think* its four-thirty? Is it four-thirty or not?"

"I don't know, but I'm sure it's tomorrow." Josephine looked unconcerned.

"So tomorrow I have to hang around church all day." Frustration appeared. Mitch needed to fire her.

"Well, yes. Sorry about that. Hey, they might move it up for you." There was that irritating wide smile as she and Hal laughed.

"All right, I'll go to the church tomorrow morning and wait until it starts."

"I'll go with you."

"That's unnecessary." I didn't need an incompetent woman

with me. I'd probably have to lead her back here.

"Suit yourself," she said it as if giving consent. I put my hand on Hal's shoulder and squeezed.

"What about Hal's funeral?"

To my relief, Hal kept quiet.

Josephine looked Hal in the eye. "A man will come and help you because of your circumstances."

"What's his name?" I asked.

"His name is Virgil," Josephine replied.

Hal moved my hand off his shoulder. His face was hard. "What's he like?"

Josephine's voice softened. "Virgil was a Knight of Malta. Do you like knights?"

Hal's face softened, but only slightly. "An actual knight?"

"Yes, he fought in the Battle of Malta in 1564."

Surprise passed through him. "1564?"

"That's right."

"When's he coming?"

"He should arrive any minute. There he is."

A man with a light of bruised blue and green hue with a hint of white arrived. She looked at him as if he needed to shower. "Josephine, the heavens are inferior to your divine silhouette."

"Good afternoon, Virgil," Josephine said.

He looked at me and asked, "Who's your friend?"

A flush of warmth passed through me as the world fell away. "My name's Dawn."

"Virgil, pleased to meet you."

I sank into his eyes and my tongue felt numb. "Likewise."

"Virgil, this is Hal." Josephine's words felt like blunt force trauma. "His funeral is tomorrow at nine a.m. at Saint Paul's United Methodist Church."

Hal clenched his jaw, eyed him warily, and took a step back.

"Hi Hal," Virgil said, and his voice softened. "How are you holding up?"

"I'm not going." Hal took another step back, and I wondered if he planned to flee.

Virgil did not approach Hal, and his body language revealed nothing. "Whether you attend your funeral is your decision. However, base it on a reason you can live with."

Hal did not reply or move.

"May I tell you about my service as a knight?"

Hal's jaw relaxed. "Okay."

To my surprise, Virgil did not talk about the Battle of Malta. Instead, he talked about his first day as a recruit. Hal laughed when Virgil said he was so ignorant, that the sergeant had to show him how to wear his uniform. Virgil told stories about his fellow soldiers and what he learned from them. He talked about their horses and how they treated them as companions. He never talked about weapons, or war, but what surprised me most was that he never talked about himself. His humility made me want to find the man inside as he ended his story.

"You lived an amazing life," Hal exclaimed.

"Thank you, but my life and their lives were amazing because we trusted each other." Virgil looked Hal in the face and made sure he understood him before changing the subject.

"Hal, I'm going to ask you to do something even though I know I must earn your trust."

Hal's response snapped the air. "You want me to attend my funeral."

"In order to live your eternal life, you must accept your earthly life. The funeral helps you do that."

Hal fought back tears as he squeezed out the words. "It

would be better for her if she didn't see me again so she can get on with her life."

"You need to say goodbye or the guilt will fester. I'll help you through it."

Hal's eyes showed me he was searching for a way out. Finding none, he surrendered. "Okay, I'll do it."

"We'll meet at the trail marker tomorrow just after sunrise," Virgil said. "We'll talk more about my life after the funeral. Would you like that?"

Hal perked up. "I would."

Virgil and Josephine left. "Good luck at the funeral," I said.

"You too," Hal replied.

The moonlight outlined nearby bushes and trees but still allowed the darkness to conceal the canyon's form. Hal's silhouette twitched, and I thought of his mother. Tomorrow he would see her face of broken glass and one day she will pass through. What happens when they meet? My thoughts entertained fantasies of Virgil only to be interrupted by my approaching funeral. Uncomfortable questions harassed me. *Who would show up? What would they say?* I sought a distraction.

"Hey, Hal, where are the pterosaurs?"

Hal started. "What?"

"The pterosaurs, where are the pterosaurs and dinosaurs? Hell Canyon should swarm with them."

"Hey, you're right. Let me think about it."

Hal stopped twitching. Seems like he also needed a distraction.

My imagination returned to Virgil. What would it be like to touch him and be touched by him? A rush of warmth, much stronger than before, surprised me. I looked down and found my shade had faded. I moved behind a bush where thoughts of my funeral intruded, which returned my shade to dark. A shout jolted me.

"I know why we're not seeing them," Hal exclaimed. His splintered light resembled a sparkler.

"OK, shoot."

"It's because we're much smaller now." It made little sense, but before I could say anything, he continued. "Picture yourself filling a glass one drop at a time." His face was excited.

"It would take forever to fill it." I said.

"That's right." He waved at the surrounding space. "The world is a giant glass and we're the drops." *We're less than dust.* "Our bodies are probably a trillionth of our original size," he said.

"That's enough," I snapped.

"They're there, but they're hard to find because they're so small." The dark skies displayed their glowing starlight, which seemed so distant that heaven seemed closer. Mr. Ferguson said the light is the last thing you see before they die. My earthly life told me I could have been running my store, keeping my boyfriend, getting married, having kids, getting rich, being President. I could have been all those things. Instead, I was in a canyon full of strangers. The night magnified my despair. *I'm not supposed to have a funeral; I'm only twenty-eight. I'm not supposed to be here.* Then, amid the recurring refrain of 'it's over', a sentence crystallized.

Tomorrow we will say goodbye for good. I wondered if daylight left for good. The memories of the lightning strike, my changed appearance, the hospital, Josephine, Hal's suicide, and the journey to Hell Canyon drowned my senses. Questions came inquiring about my grip on reality. *Am I dead? Is this happening? Am I on this river? Am I looking at a starry sky?* The darkness squeezed me with each passing minute. Hal's silhouette twitched again and his color exploded into an angry mix of purple and red. "I lost it all," he shouted. "I could have been somebody."

"We both lost it all, just under different circumstances." Tears flowed down his face as we floated in the darkness.

"I deserted her."

I tried to reassure him, but my reply sounded hollow.

"Hal, you made a mistake."

"I betrayed her."

I told him I would be there for him, no matter what. He said "thanks," but I could tell he didn't believe me. I reminded him what Josephine said.

"Maybe we lost our first chance, but Josephine said we have a second chance." Hal said he didn't deserve a second chance, which irritated me. "Well, you got one anyway. You can throw it away or make the most of it."

The darkness forced me into another question. What would the people at my funeral say about my first chance?

***

Sunrise tinted the canyon walls pink. Virgil and Josephine were talking as we approached the trail marker. Josephine had the look of a woman being pestered by a mosquito. I had to fight off the inviting warm rush upon seeing Virgil's silhouette. How could she reject this man?

"But I have some poetry I would like to recite to you. I think you'll like it," Virgil said.

"No, Virgil."

"There they are," Hal said. He advanced, but I stopped him, because I wanted to see her squirm.

"Give them a minute," I said. We sat back and watched the show.

"Why don't you give me a chance?" Virgil implored.

"Because it will not work. I'm not the woman of your dreams."

"You are. You just don't know it."

"Don't tell me what I don't know. I know plenty."

"Yes, you do, and that's one reason I'm attracted to you."

"Stop it."

Okay, Josephine, I'll take him. You're not only an incompetent searcher, but dumb. I glanced at Hal and saw his face had tightened and his shade had faded.

He still wants her after what she said to Mitch? Why doesn't he respect himself?

"Hal," I said as loudly as I dared.

Hal's face jerked, and his shade returned to normal.

"Let's go." We joined them at the trail marker.

Virgil asked me, "Are you sure you don't want Josephine to go with you?"

Waiting all day at church for my funeral was bad. Waiting all day at church with Josephine was worse. "No, thanks anyway."

Josephine looked bored. "Suit yourself."

Suddenly, I had a chance to stick it to her. "Hey Josephine, why don't you go with Virgil and Hal?"

Seeing the surprised look on Josephine's face just before the words snapped shut was beautiful to behold. "That's a great idea. It would be a pleasure to have you grace our company, Josephine," Virgil said.

"Yeah," Hal agreed.

Josephine glared at me as she ascended and left Hell Canyon

with two men she didn't like.
>   *You can't handle daddy's girl.*
> I laughed all the way to my funeral.

Chapter 4

There was the distinct cross, the simple building, the neatly landscaped grounds, and the blue and white sign that said Desert Foothills Methodist Church. It was another humid day in Phoenix, but I did not sweat nor feel thirsty. I passed through a wall and saw the chapel with its pews arranged in neat brief lines as if waiting to hear the sermon. Nothing showed a funeral would take place. I drifted back through the wall and waited. Observing the sun cross the sky was like watching paint dry. A car drove past, but it provided no relief. *Was this the eternal life, waiting around?* I looked back at the sun; it did not move.

Finally, a car pulled into the parking lot. The driver was an older man with a pale complexion. He looked like he lived his entire life behind a desk. I followed him as he unlocked the door to the chapel. He passed the pews, went to a back office, and opened a closet which contained his vestments. The man leafed through them, sliding the hangars down a wooden rail until he stopped at one that was violet colored. He closed the closet door and went to an office. A woman arrived a few minutes later. She looked like she had eaten too much at the church socials.

"When does the hearse arrive?" he asked.

"It should arrive at ten and the florists should arrive soon thereafter."

"Mr. and Mrs. Allegary arranged this pretty quickly. What time is the funeral?"

"Twelve o'clock."

So much for Josephine's reliability. Another thought intruded. *Couldn't they have waited awhile?*

A digital clock sitting on the corner of the desk said 9:37 in orange numbers. "I might as well prepare," he said.

"You've been wearing violet a lot lately."

"I could use a few weddings. Reserve the first rows for immediate family."

A shock wave rushed through me as I stumbled into the parking lot and passed through a parked hearse, which arrived early. Two men in black suits exited the hearse, flung the back door open, and eased out the coffin. Hard rubber wheels attached to stainless steel legs reached out and gripped the pavement. "That's me," I said. The words shook me like an earthquake as the men pushed the coffin inside. Mitch said it could get rough.

The florists arrived, brought the flowers inside, and left. I remained in the parking lot. No wind or other movement stirred, just the shining day. The cars arrived first in ones, then in twos, and then in a short intermittent stream before parking. Most of the people were familiar. There was Aunt Sally and Uncle Joe. There were my employees from the running store. Funny, I never saw them in shirts, ties, and dresses. They took silent, subdued strides into the chapel. An ordinary car, cleaned and waxed, came up and parked in a space up front marked 'RESERVED' in yellow letters, but the two occupants that got out were not. It was Mom and Dad, and they had that broken look only the grieving suffer. "I'll miss my little girl," Dad said.

"Please don't talk like that," Mom replied.

The ugly truth came out. *Only the past is here.* "Mom, Dad," I screamed repeatedly. "I'm still here. I'm alive." They could not hear me and I knew it, but I could not stop shouting.

"Do you think she's with us watching?" Mom asked.

"I would like to think so."

They went inside, but I did not follow. A few minutes later – maybe it was less than that – Tom, my now ex-boyfriend, arrived and entered wearing a buttoned down shirt and jacket. Shortly thereafter, Becky arrived, looking more affected than the others who came, which made sense, because she witnessed my death. She carried a manila folder and wore a black dress that looked a little short for a funeral, but I wasn't in the mood to comment. I saw the hearse and the cross and felt the depth of my fury.

Why did you kill me; I was only twenty-eight? Was it because I did not believe you existed? Was that why you took my life? There was a time I looked for you, but you stayed hidden. Did you kill me to hurt the people in the church? Was it because you thought they loved me more than you? Couldn't you let them love us both? Did you kill me because I was too sinful for you? I did the best I could. Yes, I did things I shouldn't have done, but to kill me for them?

There was only the dead wind and the bright sun.

My parents, they did right by you. Why must you make them say goodbye? Do what you like to me when I return, but let me go back for their sake.

No reply as the hearse and the cross sat in the warm air.

The funeral would soon reduce me to a memory, a story, or a photograph. I would see them, but they would not see me. I could find them, but they could never find me. Men and women inside the sanctuary prepared to make last comments about my life.

What will they say? Mom and Dad's dry voices will say I was a dutiful girl who got good grades. My relations will shift their feet and say routine things about my passing. My employees, at best, will say I was a pleasant boss. Becky will say a few words about our friendship and they will all leave. Memories of my school year showed meaningless worries over friends, boys and homework assignments. The times with Becky lacked substance. All my striving with the Running Phoenix was vanity, and the casket showed me the stupidity of my existence. *They'll say nothing about me because I blew my first chance.* I entered the church with the sun hanging over my head, dreading what they would say.

Everybody took their seats and looked away from the casket. Mom and Dad had vacant stares. Becky sat next to Tom. The minister appeared at the pulpit with a microphone and said, "Good Morning, everybody."

"Good morning," the audience murmured.

The minister began the ritual of goodbye. "We gather here today to witness the passing of Dawn Allegary."

Mitch said the funeral could be rough, but I didn't expect those words to be so painful. Seeing a tear come from Dad's eye made it worse. The minister interrupted my weeping when he offered the pulpit to those who wanted to say something. "Mr. and Mrs. Allegary will speak last," he said.

Some of my employees took the pulpit, said I was a good boss, uttered a few more words, and scooted back to their seats. Aunt Sally and Uncle Joe also came up and did the same. Could they summarize my earthly life in just a few words? Watching them quickly return to their seats disturbed me.

Becky got out of her chair. She slid past Tom and carried the manila file to the pulpit. She pulled several sheets of paper out and placed them on the lectern.

"Good morning, everybody, and thank you for coming to say goodbye to my best friend."

Oh Becky, that's so sweet.

"Before I begin, I must offer an apology to Mr. and Mrs. Allegary."

My parents sat up straight.

"Back when Dawn and I were in high school, you were concerned that I was a bad influence. Well, you were right. I tried to corrupt her in general and with boys in particular."

My parents smiled, and the audience gave an easy laugh. A grin passed across my face.

"Despite my best attempts, Dawn just didn't get boys."

What?

"That explains the lack of kids," Mrs. Allegary replied.

The crowd laughed.

Mom!

Becky gave a smile to the audience that said, 'Do you want to hear more?' before making eye contact again with my parents. Nobody replied, but she was confident she had everyone's attention when she asked my parents a question.

"Mr. and Mrs. Allegary, do you know why your daughter never wore heels?"

"No, we don't," they replied.

Becky's eyes danced. "Well, let me tell you a secret about your daughter."

Heels, what's she getting at? The crowd and my parents leaned forward.

"Please tell us," Dad said. Becky obliged.

"Dawn understood she had to dress a certain way to attract the boys. My parents called it 'playing the game.' She wore the snug shorts and the tight shirts, which got their attention, but I had to provide the adult supervision because she didn't know what to do when they came running."

Anger filled me. *You did not. It was me that provided the*

adult supervision.

The crowd chuckled, and my parents smiled. Becky waited for the laughter to fade before continuing.

"For example, Dawn liked this boy in math class, but she didn't know how to approach him. So I tried to teach her one of my tricks. I told her to ask him to help her with a math problem, although she already knew how to solve it. Then act all grateful and drop a strong hint, encouraging him to ask her out. She asks me what she should do if he doesn't know the answer."

"Ha! Ha! Ha!" the audience snickered and my angry ticked up a notch.

"One day she played the game by wearing a purple blouse, with a short white skirt, and matching heels. I remember the distinct 'wik-chuk, wik-chuck' sound they made on the sidewalk."

The skirt was not short.

Becky bobbed her torso and moved side-to-side. "She wasn't used to wearing heels. So she looked like a drunk flamingo. The heels would go wik-chuk-chuk, wik-chuck-chuck as she swayed and stumbled left and right. She looked uncomfortable, but she had a beat you can dance to."

It wasn't that bad.

The audience snickered again, and Tom had a wide grin. Again, Becky waited until all was quiet. Sunshine passed through a stained glass window.

"It was a warm November afternoon, and we were walking toward the drugstore from Mountain Pointe High School with Dawn's heels wik-chuck-wik-chucking down the sidewalk. Approaching from the opposite direction was a boy named Kyle, and the downward tilt of his head showed he noticed the long legs that reached inside that short white skirt."

I had forgotten about the heels. Now they came back to tell me what I did as shame heated my face. *Out of all the things you could have said at my funeral, you had to pick Kyle.*

"Kyle had a good heart but his face had red inflamed pimples, crevasses resembling fairway divots and a terrible affliction of blackheads and whiteheads. It looked like a three-dimensional map of the Himalaya Mountains, except without the majesty."

Becky continued her onslaught as the audience hung to every word in the still air. My head turned to Mom and Dad. *Oh my God, they're going to know.*

"There are two things that terrify a teenage girl. Boys who don't notice them and boys who notice them. Dawn's heels wobbled when Kyle said, 'Hi' in a low voice."

Some giggles came out of the crowd and others smiled as the heat in my face increased. At least Josephine wasn't here.

Becky turned over a sheet. *How many of them are there?* A sign over a door said EXIT in sharp red color, but I stayed. "But that was just the beginning of Dawn's troubles. If he had moved on, everything would have been fine. Instead, he took a deep breath, blushed and asked her if she would see a movie with him."

Why are you doing this to me? A feeling that I got what I deserved passed through me as tears slid down my face. *I'm so sorry, Kyle. I didn't know what I was doing.*

"Dawn stopped wobbling long enough to say, 'That's a big request. What makes you think you can ask me out?'"

Surprise followed by anger evicted my shame. *You said that.*

Becky enjoyed herself, which intensified my rage. "Kyle stammered and his face looked paralyzed, but he hung in there. Dawn's eyes had that panicked look. She couldn't say 'yes' but didn't know how to say 'no'. So she gave him a challenge."

Everyone looked at Becky as if she had cast a spell over them. Becky paused for so long that I expected someone to ask what the challenge was. She took a deep breath, held it for a moment and waved her finger.

"She said if you want a date with me, then go to the drugstore and buy me some tampons."

You said that, and I did not wave my finger. I understood how my humiliation would play out as the audience roared. The shame that heated my face warmed my body, and the minister grinned as if witnessing justice being meted out to Satan.

"Time appeared to freeze as Kyle wondered whether to accept her test. Dawn thought she was in the clear because no self-respecting teenage boy would dare buy tampons, but she picked the wrong day to wear the white skirt. 'I'll do it to show you I'm worth it,' he said. Dawn wobbled in her heels as she watched him march through the automatic doors."

The audience roared and Tom looked amused.

You told him to do that. A wood cross hung on a wall behind the pulpit and Becky again waited for the audience to cease laughing before she continued.

"Becky was shaking in those high heels and asked me what to do. I said, 'A teenage boy buying tampons, I don't think so. C'mon let's watch the show.' We walked in and Hal was staring at the boxes. Poor guy, those pink, blue, and red boxes marked as regular, sport, or normal confused him."

My funeral became a stand-up comedy for Becky as the audience laughed.

"Making matters, worse, the clerk came over and asked if he needed help. Kyle's face was so red you could cook food."

"Oh, no!" Some of the audience members exclaimed.

"At last, he got a box, but now he had another problem. He had to pay for them."

"Ohhhhhhh!" The audience responded, and Tom was laughing.

"He approached the cashier. We thought he would pay for them, but he put the box on his hip and ran for the exit. Dawn and her white skirt made Kyle a criminal."

"Ha! Ha! Ha! Ha!" the crowd laughed.

You encouraged him to steal them, you low-life bitch.

"He got within a few feet of the exit, when lights went on and a 'whoop-whoop' sound filled the store followed by a command." Becky brought her hand to her mouth and said with a robot voice, "Please return to the cashier and pay for the items."

Becky had to wait longer for the laughter to subside before she could continue." But then he got another command. "She said nothing, letting the tension build. Finally, when the audience appeared ready to burst, she said, "Phoenix Police Department, stop right there."

The crowd roared again, but she didn't wait for the laughter to abate. "Kyle made his run for freedom with the police officer giving chase. Dawn panicked and ran to the back of the store, with her heels tack–tack-tacking on the tile. I thought she intended to hide in the beer cooler until I heard the alarm. She went out through the emergency exit."

You told me the alarm wouldn't go off.

"I left the store and gave chase. I heard her heels wik-chucking on the pavement despite the noise. Then I heard an 'aggggh' followed by a chuck-chuck-chuck-chuck. Dawn had broken a heel."

She held an imaginary broken heel in her left hand and bobbed up and down like a football player running in choppy seas. Then in an expansive voice Becky said, "The thirty, the twenty, the ten, Touchdown!"

The audience cheered.

I should have used my good heel to pound a hole in your head. Becky finished roasting me as my silhouette radiated enough heat to start a campfire.

"I caught up with her on a street. She tore her blouse and exuded an unfeminine mixture of body odor and perfume. Her skirt was dirty, and she scraped her knee. Dawn made good her escape, but she never wore heels again."

The crowd applauded and cheered. Becky shouted, "Good luck Dawn, wherever you are. I hope you learned how to play the game."

Seeing my parents laugh completed my humiliation. Becky stepped down from the pulpit in her slutty short dress and walked down the aisle back to her seat. Tom made room for her as she put her hands on her thighs and lifted her dress slightly as she sat down. I hoped for something better as he took the pulpit.

"That was quite a story. I think there's a novel in there called *The Secret Lives of Ex-Girlfriends*," Tom said.

"Or *The Secret Lives of Daughters*," Dad yelled while Mom laughed.

How could they do that to me?

I passed under the EXIT sign and left the church angry, hurt, insulted, disrespected, and betrayed with laughter ringing in my ears. I took the rap for Becky in grade school and helped her with Math in general and Geometry in particular. She could have said that at my funeral instead of bringing up the worst day of my life. Suddenly, a fact from two days ago intervened to stop me.

Creosote bushes, and rock formations extended to the horizon. Two formations were spaced closely enough to appear as one. Snakes hid in the crevices as I recalled Becky's anguished eyes and my parents' broken faces. They saw the lightning's spider-web pattern etched on my body. Josephine's words rang out in my thoughts.

You need to say goodbye to everyone.

I turned back to Mom and Dad.

I rushed back to the church only to find the funeral had ended. An ivory silhouette of a woman giving off neutral colors floated next to a pew. "You missed your funeral," she said with a French accent.

"Who are you?"

"My name is Emily. You must be Dawn."

Who is this woman, and what is she doing at my funeral? Mistrust warned me. "My name is Martha."

Emily's voice hitched slightly. "So 'Martha', why did you come to Dawn's funeral?"

I scrambled for an answer. "Dawn was a friend of mind. I heard she passed through and hoped to find her here. Looks like I'll have to look elsewhere."

"That seems to be the case. The funeral was quite unusual."

"How so?"

"Everyone went home laughing."

***

My bruised pride and my bruised light returned to Hell Canyon. Mitch saw me as I passed some cottonwood trees at the bend in the river. "So how was the funeral?"

I acted as if my funeral was just a chore as embarrassment and idiocy teased me. "It was less than I expected."

Mitch had a perplexed look. *Is he on to me?* "Really," he

said.

I decided the best defense was a good offense. "Did I do it right? Was I supposed to feel something?" I watched his face and held my breath.

Mitch's face relaxed. "Don't worry. People react differently when they attend their funerals. Sometimes it's a delayed response."

"I'll catch you later." I moved upstream before he could respond.

The people in the group had returned with their searchers. Hal, Josephine, and Virgil were not among them. Their faces displayed mixtures of happiness and sadness as they exchanged details with each other. One of them said in a resolute voice, "I made good." A woman expressed her joy that she made the world a little better. Another man, in tears, expressed gratitude for being forgiven. "I did my best," he said.

Then a woman floated above them and said, "May I have your attention, please?" It was Norma.

"Congratulations, you made good on your first chance."

The group cheered and I wanted to hide. The man who translated for the woman yesterday beckoned me.

"A good day," he said with a Spanish accent.

"Yes, it is." I felt like an imposter.

His name was Carlos, and he worked as a janitor at the Vee Quiva casino. He cleaned the restrooms, vacuumed the gaming floor, and cleaned the gaming machines during swing shift for twenty-five years. "I provided for my daughter well enough to put her through college," he said. Her name was Awilda, and she was finishing her medical school residency at Johns Hopkins. He told me how she enjoyed working with needle and thread when she was a girl. First, her mother Beatriz taught her how to darn socks and fix tears in shirts and pants. Soon, Awilda learned how to make shirts and pants. As Awilda got older, she got a job and used the money to buy different fabrics and colors to make tablecloths and curtains of intricate patterns as she filled his house with color. Carlos thought his daughter would become a famous fashion designer and a foreign government would ask her to design a new flag, but she surprised him when she told him on her seventeenth birthday that she wanted to go to medical school. "It turned out she was a natural at stitching people." But what made him the happiest man in the eternal life was when she paid him the highest compliment at his funeral.

"Dad, you did a man's job raising me. Thanks."

I wanted to crawl into a hole when he asked how my funeral went. "They weren't ready for my sudden passing."

"I'm so sorry. I don't know how I would have handled it if it was Awilda who was here."

His kind words made me feel worse. The eternal life will know Carlos as Super *Padre* and call me *Senorita* One-Heel. The 'wik-chuk, wik-chuck' sound buzzed in my brain like a fly. He took his first chance and made a doctor. I took up space.

The group chattered and celebrated like they won a lottery as they told their stories. They interrupted each other, but everybody was too happy to take offense. One of them said words at me, but he didn't care if I listened. I eased out of the group and realized nobody knew what occurred at my funeral.

I would create my story.

It was a lie, but the eternal life would not know me as *Senorita* One-Heel. I rejoined the group and gleaned the facts from their funerals. To my surprise, the details were similar. Loving parents, siblings, and friends all describing how the deceased made their lives better.

I slipped out of the group and created my cover. The employees at my funeral waxed on about how I was a wonderful, generous, and caring boss, although I paid them minimum wage, but this was the eternal life. Nobody would know. Becky's eulogy described how she couldn't have made it through childhood without me, and my parents said that I filled their lives with joy and happiness. I kept it simple to avoid slipping up and rejoined the group.

The coffee silhouette of a man approached. "You've been quiet. Did everything go well?"

I covered my mouth. "My best friend said she couldn't have made it through childhood without me. I'm sorry it's a bit much." I recalled what I said to Carlos. "She wasn't ready for my sudden passing."

The man apologized. "I'm so sorry for failing to account for your bruised light and making it all about me. I'll leave you alone."

I can use my bruised light as a cover. "Thanks," I said, and the man moved off and gave me an excuse to be alone.

So far, my cover was successful, but I was sure Josephine would apply a stronger test. A brief scan of my surroundings showed only the cliffs, trees, and some birds in flight. I silently rehearsed what to say. My employees said I was a great boss. My best friend said she couldn't make it through childhood without me, and my parents said I filled their lives with joy and happiness.

What if Josephine asks how I got Becky through childhood? I would say, 'I don't know. That's what she said.' I watched the edge of the canyon and waited while the group and their searchers chatted.

Hal, Josephine, and Virgil returned, passing over trail marker

#9012. Virgil and Josephine had grim looks while Hal looked shattered.

"She said it was her fault," Hal wept.

"I'll help you through it," Virgil said.

"I'm going to have to live with this for the rest of my life," Hal screamed and his face twisted.

Dread filled me. "Hal, what happened?"

"Not now," Josephine waved me off.

Hal yelled at me." What do you think happened?"

I never had the misfortune of attending such a funeral, but it wasn't hard to figure out. Those attending Carlos' funeral would pay tribute to a man who gave his life to others in general and his daughter in particular. Those attending Hal's funeral would labor to find awkward words for a boy who induced his own death. Awilda said her father did a man's job. What could Hal's mother say?

"Hal, I know it's rough now, but you completed the first step, which was crucial," Virgil said.

"She thinks it's her fault." The guilt made Hal want to die all over again.

I recalled my promise to protect him. "Hal, you made a mistake. You need our help."

"Shut up," Josephine said.

That incompetent bitch. Hal spoke again, interrupting my outrage.

"I was not true to the one person who was in my corner during my earthly life. It would've been far better to be murdered instead."

An awkward silence followed. I didn't know whether to leave or stay as neither seemed right. At last, Virgil moved next to Hal.

"You did a hard thing. Now would you like to hear something about my life? I promised you that."

"Yes," Hal muttered.

The wind shook the trees and agitated the river with angry ripples. Gray clouds and the smell of rain approached from the horizon while dust swirled on top of Hell Canyon and the sun vanished.

"I had been a knight for two years. We were engaged in a battle with the Turks on the Adriatic Sea near a town called Tivat. The Turks had been raiding the coastal towns for years, and the Pope sent us to stop them. The sun baked us mercilessly on that glassy sea as we fought from early morning to twilight. I never thought water could taste so good. We were relieved when the sun finally set and the cool breeze arrived."

The wind and clouds arrived, but there was no rain, though I could smell it. The river rose in a matter of minutes and the cliffs disappeared in a curtain of gray. Virgil's story rose above the sound of the wind, and I observed Josephine had left.

"We had to disengage because the night would make it too dark to see and the fleet had to return to Malta for water. Unfortunately, while disengaging from the Turks, the Admiral turned into their artillery fire, which resulted in two sunk galleys and many drowned sailors."

Virgil said that many sailors died of heatstroke while returning to Malta. When they arrived two days later, they found everyone surprised to see them. It turned out the residents of Tivat concluded the Turks sunk the fleet when they saw bodies and debris floating in the harbor the next day. Virgil smiled. "Their messengers were very prompt in delivering the message which goes to show that the only thing that travels faster than bad news is wrong news."

"I thought knights just fought on land," Hal said.

Virgil's smile remained unchanged. "When you're a knight, you fight where they send you."

Hal looked at Virgil intently. I realized he never mentioned his dad, who probably didn't attend the funeral.

"Why didn't you get water at Tivat?" Hal asked.

"The Turks could have pinned us in the harbor." Spheres of silver raindrops passed between us and splashed the ground as the river swelled its banks. The wind died off and sunlight appeared in the southwest as the gray clouds passed over the cliffs. The river crested, and the storm abated a few minutes later. Virgil finished his story.

"The military tribunal relieved him of command because of the lost galleys, but he didn't give up. He remained in Malta and took an assignment which required him to maintain the munitions for the fleet. He did a superb job and regained command of the fleet two years later."

Hal maintained the intent look. "That's so awesome."

Visions of romance swirled in my head as I pictured myself with him on a Maltese beach.

Virgil looked Hal square in the eye. "You and that Admiral have something in common."

Hal eyes became confused. "What are you talking about, Virgil? He commanded ships. I'm nobody special."

Virgil didn't let up. "That Admiral faced up to the Tribunal. You faced up to your funeral. He could have run, but he didn't. You could have run but didn't. You have man in you, Hal, and we need to bring it out."

Did any man ever talk to him this way? I couldn't imagine his mother or any woman saying such words.

Hal still looked confused. "I do?"

"We build tomorrow. See you at the trail marker," Virgil said.

Hal's splintered light gave off a bubbling bright blue and green, which he subdued when he noticed me. He put on his deep voice. "Yeah, see you tomorrow."

It was just the two of us. The river returned to its normal level, but a tree snagged on some boulders, which affected its flow.

"Looks like you have a big day tomorrow," I said.

"Yeah." He practiced camouflaging himself inside the brown branches of a nearby bush. At first, his brown was darker than the branch, then slowly lightened until it matched. He was learning to control his chameleon light.

I needed an excuse to leave so he wouldn't have to ask about my funeral. "I need to find Mitch, I'll catch you later."

"See you." He ignored me as he kept practicing.

It wasn't thirty seconds after I left when I heard someone say, "There you are." It was Mitch floating in front of Trail Marker #9012. I waited for him to speak, concerned that he would ask more questions about my funeral. Instead, he gave me another assignment.

"Two members from the Association of Botanists are coming tomorrow, so please attend."

"Who are they?"

He said their names were Phil and Willie, who worked as field botanists for Monsanto. As he spoke, I considered if he had tracked Josephine's movements earlier than the Verde River. He could have watched her find me at the hospital and Hal at his home and the chameleon light would camouflage him, but there was no evidence he did.

"Don't be a sap and see what they have to say," Mitch said.

I ignored his pun. "OK, I'll be there. Where do I meet them?"

"Trail Marker #9012, everybody meets there."

He left, and I tailed him. He moved up to a high tree, and I found a higher tree to watch him. I stayed behind the trunk and waited. The sun set and twilight came and went, but he remained. I could see the faint silhouettes nearby, members of my group. Then, as the last rays of sundown vanished, a woman's bruised silhouette appeared. It was Patricia.

Mitch's silhouette changed to orange, and his shade faded. "Glad you could make it."

Patricia's shade faded, and her silhouette changed to pink. "I just can't get enough of your pleasure."

"They've gotten larger since the last time."

"Your hands bring out the best in my girls."

I tried cynicism to medicate the aching void of loneliness yawning inside me as they kissed. *He's building up your heart only to destroy it utterly and completely. Did he tell you that you were the only one? Are you dumb enough to believe it?*

Becky's words from my funeral invaded my eternal life. *Good luck, Dawn, wherever you are. I hope you learned how to play the game.* Was I still the dumb fifteen-year-old girl wobbling in heels?

My head warned me to stay because I had spoken to Patricia earlier, but the pain of their intimacy drove me off. Thoughts of Virgil tormented me as I passed through the trees. Some silhouettes from my group gathered at the tree snag on the river. Their bubbling happiness magnified the loneliness. I moved under a rock to suffer in silence, but it made things worse. A light downstream flickered on, then off, as if it was signaling airline traffic. It was Hal, and he had become fixated on his chameleon light. My promise to protect him suppressed the ache I was suffering.

"How's it going?" I asked.

"All right," he said. His light kept flickering.

He returned to the river carrying a load of guilt from his funeral. I considered confronting him, but that could mean telling him about my funeral. *Senorita* One-Heel needed to stay buried. The silhouettes with their unbruised and un-splintered lights upstream chattered like happy birds.

"Hal, listen to me. We're different, so we gotta pull together. If something happens to you, I'm alone."

Hal's light steadied. "What do you mean?" he asked, but his voice understood me.

I pointed upstream. "We don't have normal colors like they do."

"You're right. Yours is bruised while mine is splintered."

I recalled Patricia. "There's one other person, and she's a searcher. Her name is Patricia, and she has a bruised light."

"Can we trust her?"

Would she tell Mitch about our earlier conversation? She didn't want me to say anything, but that meant nothing. "I don't know."

Hal clutched me the way a scared toddler clutches his mother. "I fear tomorrow."

"Likewise." The ache stayed away as I held him. A minute passed and new words came. "Remember this. No matter how bad things get, you have someone in the eternal life."

CHAPTER 5

The group looked at Hal's splintered light with judgmental looks. My light did not reveal my sin but I knew Kyle and my parents would pass through one day.

Hal, I, and the rest of the group met Mitch and Virgil at Trail Marker #9012. Josephine and two other searchers arrived, leading a large group of scared and confused men and women. None of them had bruised or splintered lights.

"Another forty-eight, we're at capacity now," Mitch said.

"Capacity?" I asked.

"People pass through every day but we can only take so many. These associations come in to find new members which helps keep our numbers manageable."

"So Hell Canyon's a terminal," I said.

"That's right. People stay here until they decide it's time to leave. Usually, they depart pretty quickly."

The Society was too busy finding dates, locations, and times for other funerals to care about my mine, but I recalled Mitch's perplexed look when I returned. He had to be suspicious. I had to leave but I was new to the eternal life.

Phil arrived, but Willie did not. Phil did not explain why Willie did not make it. Mitch sounded like a game show host when he introduced him. "Everybody, this is Phil, who is a member of the Botany Association. Phil, can you tell us a little about yourself?"

Phil was in his second year as a member of the Association.

In his earthly life, he worked in the pesticides division for the Monsanto Corporation. His colleagues called him 'Chlor-O-Phil' and it was his job to understand how pesticides affected plants. "It's bad form to destroy a farmer's crop yield." His ivory silhouette chuckled. "Follow me into that tree."

"Get going," Mitch said. We followed Phil into the tree, except for Hal, who left with Virgil.

Sap ran through the tree's veins, rising for the branches. The veins spread through the tree in an intricate lattice. What beauty I saw, but I had no language to tell it.

"Beautiful, isn't it? I'll show you how the sap rises later today," Phil said. "Now, let's leave the tree for a moment and gather at a leaf, where I'll tell you how chlorophyll works."

"Show, don't tell," somebody said.

"Ah, a writer in the group." We regrouped at a leaf. "Does anybody know why this leaf is green?"

We didn't answer.

"Come with me then." We followed him into the leaf. Phil pointed to cells resembling sliced cucumbers. "That's the chloroplast where the chlorophyll is located." He led us into the chloroplast and pointed to the green color. "That's the chlorophyll. It's green because it reflects the light's green wavelength."

The chlorophyll released a clear substance.

Phil looked like a proud father. "The chlorophyll converts carbon dioxide and sunlight into this clear liquid called glucose or sugar, which is used to create new plant parts. You knew it in high school as photosynthesis."

I couldn't believe we were inside a cell watching this. Mitch said there was a whole world to explore but I did not expect this.

"This is better than a microscope," somebody exclaimed.

"Yeah," somebody else replied.

"I always messed up the slides," a third person responded.

Phil displayed to us how the sugar moved from the leaves to the trunk. It was like watching a network of rivers. Forty-eight of us watched in amazement as the sugars, water, and minerals rushed past. Then the businesswoman in me whispered, "There's a price."

"I'll be outside the tree, if you have questions," Phil said. I don't think they heard him. He had a contented smile as I joined him.

"What's the price?" I asked.

A surprised and confused look passed across his face. "What do you mean what's my price?"

The businesswoman in me told me to be tough. "Are you telling me that you're doing this out of the goodness of your heart?"

Phil gave me a stern look. "The only thing I had when I passed through was the forty-three years of knowledge I gained studying plants and trees. A woman named Sophia said I could jail the learning in my head or free it for others. As to price, what do you think I can sell?"

"Membership to your club."

"They can join me if they want, but understanding life requires a willingness to learn." He emphasized the next sentence. "Show don't tell. Whoever said that taught me something." He returned to the group without bothering to see if I followed.

Mitch said other societies were coming to Hell Canyon. Should I leave with this group now or should I stay? Leaving would mean deserting Hal and betraying my promise to him that he had someone no matter how bad things got. I stayed.

Late afternoon came and three members of our group told Phil they wanted to join the Botany Association. "My pleasure." Our group dispersed, and I returned to trail marker #9012.

As I looked at the marker, I recalled the clearing where Josephine looked directly at Hal and me. She had to have seen our lights glowing. Not moving was the only thing that saved us. I then recalled Mitch's skill in blending in with the bush and concluded I had to learn to use the chameleon light. I moved to the marker and practiced.

Changing my color to match the marker was harder than it looked. My first attempts resembled splashed paint just like Hal's. A closer look revealed I did not account for the marker's shades of brown, with some shades light enough to approach white and other shades dark enough to approach black. I was just getting the hang of it when a voice surprised me.

"It's been two days since you passed through and you're already hiding?" Patricia said. Norma was floating next to her chuckling.

I chose my words carefully, aware Patricia was close to Mitch. "Mitch was showing the chameleon light to Hal so I decided to try it out."

"We prefer men to see us so we can make their hearts thump," Norma said.

"Can't do that with the chameleon light," Patricia replied.

"Point taken," I said.

Virgil and Hal arrived. Hal had the look of a boy coming home from a good day at school as his splintered light gave off bubbling blue and green colors. I pictured Virgil and me as husband and wife with Hal as our son. A fleeting warmth told me to make his heart thump.

"See you here tomorrow," Virgil said.

The sound of his words stoked my desire to make him stay but I let him leave without saying a word. Becky's last words from my funeral gave me a fresh sting. *I hope you learned how to play the game.* A fresh sting followed. *That explains the lack of kids.*

"I'll be here." Hal's voice beamed with enthusiasm as Virgil left.

Norma and Patricia looked uncomfortable. "We'll see you tomorrow," Norma said.

"Bye," I replied.

After they left, Hal said, "They don't like me." A resigned look replaced the enthusiasm.

"How do you know?" I already knew the answer because Norma and Patricia's faces had the same look as the group that saw Hal leave with Virgil that morning.

"It's easy to figure out," he said.

I changed the subject. "So how was your first day with Virgil?"

His words spilled out and his enthusiasm returned. "Virgil's amazing. He told me about the Battle of Malta and how he made friends with Turgat, after they passed through."

I expected him to deliver a monologue on male bonding. "Really."

"But get this, Turgat was his enemy."

"Interesting."

Hal kept going. "He explained why I had to love my enemies."

That's when I remembered the fight Dad and I had.

We were watching the news when the newscaster said a judge sentenced a man to twenty-five years for rape. I said, "I hope he's their bitch." He said I had no right to wish suffering on others. I told him that man would have come after me. The more we argued, the wider the gulf became. The following Sunday would be the last time I attended church.

I looked Hal in the eye and said, "What did Virgil say about loving your enemy?"

Hal's words were all over the place. "He said Matthew told him we're enemies because our leaders say we're enemies. Then he said Turgat and he brought them together on an island after they passed through at the battle of Malta. There they helped make friends between the Janissaries and the Knights of Malta."

"Hal, let's start over."

I had to stop him every second sentence with a question to understand him. Virgil perished at Fort Saint Michael during the Battle of Malta from Turkish cannon fire. Matthew was a searcher and a priest, who was there when Virgil passed through. Further questions revealed Matthew and other searchers were performing war service. "Virgil said they were passing through by the hundreds," Hal said. I felt a wave of respect for Josephine as I recalled Mitch's reference to her war service at the clearing. How many soldiers did she comfort after they passed through? How many second chances did she offer? How many funerals did she arrange for them to attend?

"Okay Hal, let me get this straight. Virgil passed through at Fort Saint Michael. Matthew is a searcher and a priest, who performed war service."

"That's right." His blue and green colors emphasized his excitement.

"What happened next?"

Hal said that Matthew took Virgil and his fellow knights over the ocean, where they saw the silhouettes of strange fish and foreign birds. They arrived at a nearby rocky island with wind-bent trees and scarce beach and soon met the men they had been fighting. More searchers joined Matthew, who formed a barrier between the two groups.

Hal skipped ahead. "Turgat was a Janissary."

I slowed him down again. "Wait a minute. What happened after the searchers formed a barrier?"

Hal said Matthew told the men they were stripped down to basic creation, no uniform or rank, only the status of male and that their character was their only possession in the eternal life. Hal's colors bubbled and brightened when he explained how Matthew also told them they could continue to be enemies but would not gain or defend the air, land, or sea. Hal's chest puffed out when he said, "Leave now if you want to continue your war."

"Did they leave?"

"Did who leave?"

"Did some of the soldiers leave to continue the war?"

"Oh yeah, some did."

"What about the ones who stayed?"

"Oh yeah, they learned about the Society of Searchers but they stayed to themselves." Hal stopped.

Frustration was building as I suppressed the urge to hit Hal upside the head but I forced myself to be patient.

"So how did Virgil and Turgat become friends?"

Hal's words became more organized after I had him explain that a Janissary was a Turkish soldier. Hal said that the day before Virgil and Turgat met, Matthew told them that if they want to make good on their second chance, they had to reconcile what they did with their first chance. Virgil told Matthew he wanted to reconcile his first chance by making friends with his enemies but did not know what to say.

"That's when Matthew said, 'Maybe the Lord will put some

words in your mouth.'" Hal's excitement showed he was about to go off track again. I asked him another question.

"What happened the next day?"

"That's the coolest part."

Hal described the day Virgil and Matthew approached the Janissaries. Virgil said he had a question and asked Matthew to translate but Matthew asked for one of the Janissaries to interpret. One of them agreed to do so. Hal tried to imitate Virgil and his face showed excitement. "Who shot the cannon that killed me?"

Hal had trouble containing himself. "But get this, the man didn't reply. Virgil asked if he should rephrase his question but the man said he should he ask a different question."

The urge to hit him resurfaced. "What happened next, Hal?"

"He said, 'I just wanted to say 'good shooting'."

I had to wait for Hal to stop laughing to confirm Turgat was the translator and was about to write it off as an irritating case of male bonding, when Hal said something surprising.

"Virgil said he would never have learned about Turkish customs and met so many interesting people if they had remained enemies. He said you have to love your enemies because you don't truly know who they are."

He has connections? I tried to act like I didn't care. "Are you saying Virgil knows people?"

"Oh yeah, he has friends all over the world."

With Virgil, I could ditch my past. Dreams of him taking me to foreign lands and introducing me as his girl cropped up as my chest expanded. Then Hal burst my fantasy balloon.

"Then we talked about Josephine."

An unpleasant image of her, Virgil, and Hal emerged. The fact this incompetent burned out searcher dismissed me as daddy's money and didn't like Virgil made her more disgusting yet he wanted her. He was there for the taking but I had to break that witch's spell she had on him. Hal's mouth kept moving but I didn't hear a word. I would take Virgil and show her naked foolishness to the world.

I hope you learned how to play the game.
Game on.

All I needed was a plan to break her spell.

A question confronted me. *Would you take Virgil if it means betraying Hal?*

I pushed it aside.

"Hi Josephine," Virgil's voice had that sad puppy sound.

"Hi Virgil," Josephine responded with annoyed politeness as she moved toward another part of the river.

"Hi Virgil," Hal said with an eager voice.

Watching Hal and Virgil leave, I realized finding the plan to break Virgil's attraction to Josephine was harder than it looked. Somehow, I had to get in his head and open his eyes. I practiced blending in with the paint on Trail Marker #9012 but became bored and left to attend the League of Physicists' presentation.

The number within our group dwindled with each passing day. Four men joined the Order of the Military Veterans and two women joined the Chemistry Club. Carlos taught me some Spanish but he also left. The newcomers came but did not stay long just like Mitch said. Soon, Hal was the only familiar face and I was relieved to see him every time he returned to the trail marker.

However, Hal's initial enthusiasm had vanished and he became more quiet and withdrawn. Recalling my promise to protect him, I asked him if he was all right.

"Virgil wants me to make friends." Panic and agitation flashed in his eyes.

"That doesn't sound so bad."

Hal's color changed to red. "They're not worth it."

I recalled Norma and Patricia's choice to avoid him. "Some people are worth it."

"Take a look around."

Feeling cornered, I gave in. "It's your choice. You don't have to do it."

"Damn right I don't."

I bet you don't yell at Virgil. Was he yelling at me because I was a woman or because he could trust me? The tension eventually diminished but not the doubt.

***

Some sunrises had clouds, others wind, rain, or snow but most only had a bright pink light. As each sunrise passed, the lonelier I felt. The recently passed through would arrive, stay a day or two, join a society, and leave. It was like trying to make friends at an airport. Hal and I still talked but it was not the same any more and Virgil barely looked at me. One day, while waiting at the trail marker, Hal and Virgil had not returned.

The sun's position showed daylight was getting short. I saw a man, who I recognized earlier as a searcher, and asked him if he knew where Virgil was. He pointed to a nearby cliff. A large reddish-brown piece appeared ready to fall.

"He should be over there. I think he's with someone."

I thanked him and left. As I approached the cliff, I heard voices. Using my chameleon light, I sneaked in only to find two men talking, one of which I deduced was a counselor.

"I can go anywhere without worry about money, eating, shelter, or health and talk to the most learned men and women. I can make friends with unfamiliar people without concern for circumstance but I would give it up to taste a beer again. Have you forgotten the nice nutty dark taste and its cold pleasant flow through your throat? What I'd give to taste the salt on tortilla chips and the sting of a hot salsa."

"The only thing I can say is that your friends will eventually join you," the counselor replied. "And yes, there are days I miss the cold taste of a beer and the salt and sting of chips and salsa."

I moved on. The cliff faced looked more eroded and the sandstone showed it was chipped as I neared it. Hal and Virgil's voices filled the air accompanied by the scent of flowers. I made sure my chameleon light was at the proper shade as I camouflaged myself with a nearby leaf.

Squared shoulders and an expanded chest marked Virgil's posture. "Hal, you've got to make friends with people who aren't like you. It's key to building your life."

Hal's light turned black. "I see how they look at me."

Virgil continued to press. "Your black glow shows you find my advice threatening, why?"

"I just told you."

A gust of wind passed through. "Hal, do you think the Janissaries suddenly loved me when I made friends with Turgat? It takes grit and willpower to do this, but you're going to find the eternal life a lonely place if you don't."

Hal's light remained dark. Virgil then gave Hal a harder task. "You're going to need to do another thing."

Hal's black hue took a darker shade. "What's that?"

"For you to build your eternal life, you must look within and find why you decided to end your earthly life."

Hal's glow flashed. "I told you bullies afflicted me and my father deserted me."

Virgil maintained an imperturbable calm. "Hal, other men and women have suffered these things but they did not kill themselves. I understand mental illness and persecution can cause suicide but there's no evidence of that. Other people sacrifice themselves to save another but that's not suicide. You need to look within and find the truth about yourself."

Hal said nothing.

"Your mother will eventually pass through and one day the two of you will meet. You owe her an explanation. How are you going to pay her?"

"I'm not going to meet her."

"Everybody meets everybody in the eternal life."

The thought of meeting Kyle chilled my silhouette.

Virgil ended the discussion. "Okay Hal, I've given you a lot to think about. Let's talk some more tomorrow but tonight remember this. When you decide to look within yourself, I'll help you see."

Hal bolted. Virgil gazed at the canyon wall for a moment, looked in my direction, and left.

To my surprise, I reached the trail marker ahead of Hal, who arrived a minute later. We left without saying a word. His hue changed to a neutral color upon seeing me but the colors looked strained.

"How did it go?" I asked.

"Fine," he mumbled.

We went to an overlook as sunset came with shades of pinks, reds and orange. Hal soon left without saying a word and I pretended to be preoccupied with the soft light bathing the river, trees, and cliffs. Slowly but surely, the stars arrived. Suddenly, a rumble startled everyone.

"What was that?" a panicked voice yelled.

Mitch's soothing voice wafted through the air. "Not to worry, the cliff face broke off."

Random thoughts passed through my mind as the sound ebbed. Without warning, a memory of Virgil's squared shoulders, expanded chest, and his shade appeared. The memory changed to fantasy as his shade disappeared revealing him in full. A burning lust seized me showing me how I can touch him and squeeze him in the right place, in the right way, at the right time. Then it showed what he could do for me and to me.

"Get him," the lust demanded.

My glow changed to a hot pink and my shade vanished, revealing me in full as visions of Patricia and Mitch flashed. Fearing someone would see me, I tried to suppress it but the color would not yield. I hid in the crevice of a rock where passion's hunger tormented me. Is this what insanity is like?

We build up a man's heart only to destroy it utterly and completely.

Who were his connections?

***

Hal did not return.

The usual sunrise came to Hell Canyon. I went to Trail Marker #9012 thinking he was there. Virgil arrived and we were alone, which gave me a fleeting chance.

Get him.

I needed to make him feel comfortable as an aggressive move might make him flee. Fortunately, I knew what to do. This girl knows how to hunt.

I flashed just enough smile to get his attention. "Tell me, Virgil, why do you do this work?"

Virgil replied as if everybody asked him this question. "I saw a lot of maimed men as a knight. After I passed through, I decided to make it my life's work to fix people."

"Do you think you can fix Hal?"

"Here's the rub. Hal must also fix himself."

The smile came off my face as I suppressed my frustration. The look on Virgil's face told me I was no closer to getting him.

The trail marker's shadow shortened as the sun ascended. It became clear Hal was not coming.

"I better tell Mitch," Virgil said. He was about to leave when Mitch arrived.

"Virgil, you're still here at the trail marker," Mitch said.

"Looks like we have a runner," Virgil said.

Mitch responded casually. "I'll look in the usual places."

I deduced what Virgil said but I did not know what Mitch meant. "The usual places?" I asked.

Mitch explained. "This is probably what happened. Virgil told Hal some hard truths. During the night, Hal decided to leave and probably didn't say goodbye. After wandering about, he met some of his fellow splinters and decided to join them."

"I did tell him some hard truths," Virgil said.

I felt a sense of guilt. "Splinters?"

Mitch nodded to Virgil before replying, "It's the term we use for those who have splintered lights."

"Are you going to bring him back?"

Mitch's face became stern. "It's his choice."

A tether within me snapped releasing a trickle of panic. "He's only a boy."

"He'll come back when he stops running from himself."

"You're just going to leave him at their mercy." The trickle became a stream.

"Dawn, they can't hold him against his will." Mitch grabbed my arm, surprising me, but I easily escaped. "See what I mean." He ascended out of the canyon leaving me with Virgil at the trail marker.

"I'm sorry it didn't work out," I said.

"I've been doing this for centuries. Sometimes you succeed. Sometimes you fail," Virgil replied.

We floated awkwardly, as an uncomfortable silence encroached. Finally, Virgil spoke.

"Guess I'll hang around here awhile until I get the next assignment."

"The next assignment?"

"Someone will come by and request my services." He said it with the attitude of a man who knows he's the best in his field.

Mitch returned. "Just as I thought, he's with his fellow splinters."

The stream flowed faster. "We need to get him back."

"As I said before, he'll come back when he stops running from himself," Mitch said.

I recalled my oath. "I promised I'd protect him."

"You can't protect him," Virgil said.

"Lead me to them," I implored Mitch.

Mitch's face looked like stone. "Dawn, there's nothing you can do."

The stream intensified. "Please."

"No."

I left the canyon going the direction Mitch had taken. A forbidding trackless desert of cactus, Palo Verde trees, and creosote bushes stretched west. A patch of green on the trunk of a nearby Palo Verde tree had a darker shade. Thinking Hal was camouflaging himself, I called out to him.

"Hal, is that you?"

There was no response or movement. Either it was part of the tree or Hal had gotten very good at using his chameleon light.

The splinters had to be nearby but, unlike Mitch, I had no idea where to look. At first, I tried to conduct a grid search to find Hal, but quickly lost patience and zigzagged about to no effect. How long was Hal wandering before they found him? What was he thinking? The sun was at its zenith when a man with a splintered red glow approached.

He had a bronze silhouette similar to Josephine's color and glared at me. "What are you doing here?"

His challenge caught me off guard for an instant but I answered him with hard words of my own. "What do you mean what am I doing here? You don't own this place."

"I've been watching you wander about for a while." He pointed to a cliff. "Hell Canyon is on the other side."

Hoping he might be able to help me, I told him what I was seeking. "I'm looking for a boy named Hal."

"We already told Mitch he was with us. We're done here." The man began to turn away but I got in his face.

"Not so fast, I made Hal a promise and I'm going to keep it."

He gave me a long look. "What's your promise?"

"I'd protect him."

"He's safe now. Now get out of here."

"Not so fast. I need him to say it."

He gave me a hard stare, which I returned. He still gave off the red glow but it had diminished. "Wait here."

The sun moved past its zenith and I wondered if he conned me. At last, Hal arrived. Awkward words followed and we avoided eye contact.

"Are they treating you all right?"

He gave a one-word reply. "Yeah."

"I looked for you because I gave you my word."

He gave another one-word reply. "Thanks."

I had nothing left to say except goodbye and good luck. The panic welled up. "Hal, you can still come back."

"No."

"You can learn so much."

"Go back over the cliff, Dawn."

The words I struggled to suppress forced themselves out. "Good luck, Hal."

"You too." And the only person I knew left.

No matter how bad things get, you have someone in the eternal life.

I had no one.

The creosote bushes, palo verde trees, and cactus seemed to stare at me. Menacing images of Bosch's, Goya's and Bruegel the Elder's paintings confronted me. Something within me broke its restraint and sent me reeling. The last thing I remembered before I screamed was the sensation of free fall.

The screaming may have lasted thirty seconds or thirty minutes but it left me emotionally stripped when it ended. A voice from within gave an urgent command.

Find your parents.

I had someone in the earthly life.

***

The familiar city sounds of Phoenix gave me comfort and soon I saw their house and the promise of safety. The garden bloomed with red, purple, and yellow flowers and gave off a pleasing fragrance as water flowed from a hose. Bees moved from petal to petal covered in pollen, their wings beating hard. I passed through the wall.

The flat screen television in the living room was off. There was the carpeting and its familiar gray-black pattern. The sun bathed Wheels, who was sleeping on the window sill. Pictures of me adorned the walls. One showed me in cap and gown. Another showed me as a girl sitting at a picnic table at Bryce Canyon. A cloth of red and white squares and bowls and plates of potato salad, hamburgers, and pickles covered the table. But my parents were not there.

The memory of hamburgers, fries, beer, onions, pickles, lemon meringue pie, chocolate ice cream, and a jar of hot mustard, sitting in the grocery cart rushed back in vivid colors. *Tom, of course. I'll go there. Love will find a way.* I remembered the kiss that told him to unhook my bra. Tears came as I rushed outside and headed for his house.

I arrived at his place and entered through the closed window, the glass briefly showing its liquid interior. Pots and pans soaking in dishwashing soap filled the kitchen sink. A calendar hung on the wall, showing it was March.

How could it be March? I passed through on twelve August . I wondered what day it was as the calendar gave me thirty-one-days to choose. Water churned in the dishwasher and the clean kitchen counter displayed an open wine bottle and two wineglasses. *How did so much time pass? How could I not observe the seasons' change?* One of the wine glasses had lipstick on it. A noise came from the bedroom: "Oh my God! Oh my God! Oh my God!" It was a woman's voice.

Becky? Still confused about my lost sense of time, I entered.

There on the bed was my boyfriend, Tom, and my best friend Becky with Tom on top doing what a man does.

"Oh my God! Oh my God! Oh my God!" Becky repeated. It changed to a duet with Tom grunting and Becky squealing as if she needed oiling. Their sounds slowly decreased to soft waves before reaching eventual silence.

There on the floor were her white shorts and maroon t-shirt, both used to great effect. A white bra and a pair of white panties lay next to them. 'You got to wear a white bra and white panties,' she told me once in the high school locker room. 'It makes men think you're a virgin.'

"You're so much woman," Tom said. He had a silly smile as he grunted and rolled off.

He never said that to me. A hurt welled up.

"And you're so much man," Becky said. She had the same stupid smile.

Becky enjoyed the attention as he squeezed her breasts and ran his fingers over her nipples. The hurt intensified as they touched in the way that used to be mine.

"I love you and your bad girl ways," Tom said with that silly smile.

He never said that to me either.

"Another man captured by my feminine powers." She returned his silly smile with one of her own.

"Do you know what that black dress of yours contained?" He asked.

"No." Becky's eyes widened in anticipation.

"A magic girl."

He never said that to me.

"Oh Tom, you make it so much fun to be a woman." Becky beamed. She shifted her position, showing more of her.

"I must confess that I made one slight lie to you." He stood up.

"You better explain yourself," she said with fake anger.

"You know when I saw you at the funeral I told you it was when you took your seat that got my attention?" His smile curled.

"Yes." Her eyes widened again.

"Actually, it was when you raised your dress and opened your legs when you sat down." He said it softly, with a hint of guilt.

"It took some positioning to make sure you saw it." Her smile widened. "I almost flashed the minister. Easy to do because it's a nightclub dress."

You traitorous bitch, I should have bashed a hole in your head with my good heel. Anger mixed into the wound.

"You need a spanking," Tom said. She laughed and squealed, dodging his reach and leaping off the bed. She ran into the bathroom where he followed. Then a soft whack followed by a laugh followed by another whack and a squeal. The sound of water flowed from the shower and the squealing subsided. Tom said, "Now let me take wonderful care of you."

He never said that either. The wound opened some more.

"But I'm such a naughty girl."

"How does a naughty girl feel so nice?"

"Gymnastics." The water played on as I cracked.

There was the bed which he once offered to me. *How could you betray me, Tom?*

A new voice jarred me. "What's with the rage Dawn?" It was Josephine.

"Mawwrrrrr!" Plus Tourner.

Seeing her was like seeing the devil. Becky's words at my funeral jolted me.

Good luck Dawn, wherever you are. I hoped you learned how to play the game.

I blew my first chance.

Chapter 6

A purple hue mixed with a tint of red flowed from me as my chest ached from anger and hurt. Before I could respond, Josephine gave me a sad look before Tourner's question-mark tail got her attention.

"Tourner, quitte á se lécher les des chaussures." Tom's clothes were on the floor and Tourner was sniffing something inside his shoes when he stopped.

Her presence aggravated my anger. "What's with the rage? What's with the rage? I'll tell you what the rage is. My boyfriend and my best friend are doing each other."

Josephine looked at me like a parent. "Dawn, you know the part of the marriage vow that says 'until death do you part'."

I glared at her and shouted, "Get to the point or shut up."

"You understand the marriage ends when husband or wife dies?"

"Yes." My eyes bore down on her.

"It applies here too." Her face expressed no emotion as I felt the knockout blow of her verbal punch.

"I'm his naughty girl and should be in the shower with him. I'm the one who's so much woman. She has no business taking him," I gasped.

Josephine verbally punched me again. "I know you should be in that shower, but you passed through and when you pass through the rules change."

"Why did this happen to me?" The shower turned off and

their happy sounds cut me deeply and the rumpled bed and the disordered pillows stung my eyes. Josephine gazed at the bathroom with a sad, distant, faraway look. "Why don't we continue this outside?" She said with a sharp voice. "Tourner."

Doubt assailed me as we went outside and the image of Becky's black dress returned. "She used my funeral to fish for men, my boyfriend."

Josephine gave an approving look. "Well, I have to admit that was enterprising of her."

"Enterprising, do you think this is funny?" I moved toward her.

She raised her hands. "No, no, I don't think it's a joke, but they must keep living."

"He should have waited for me."

Her voice took on a professorial tone. "Are you saying he should not see another woman?"

The stupidity of my statement was obvious so I used anger to hide my embarrassment. "Ummm, nohhh. My funeral, really?"

"Dawn, life goes on."

Josephine's voice changed to a detective's tone. "This should be easy to guess. You tried to return to your earthly life because the eternal life got rough. You probably ran to your parents before running to your boyfriend, but found out the hard way, pardon the pun that he moved on with his life."

Tom's blue car and Becky's red car sat in the driveway. Gray clouds approached, offering rain. Blasts of wind bent the trees and the street pavement changed to a deeper black. Josephine's voice pierced the wind. "Do you remember when I told you there were people who could answer why you passed through?"

I looked at her like a little boy, whose mistake cost his team the game. "Yeah, you said that when my cat was starving. I can use some answers."

Josephine moved close to me. "How about we leave this happy couple alone and work on your second chance?"

Surrender washed through me. "Okay."

Josephine's eyes narrowed. "Her name is Ester and she stays in Omaha, Nebraska and you need a change of scenery. I'll need to let Mitch know." I never thought much about Omaha, Nebraska, but then who did? An insurance company, a football team, steaks; Rosenblatt Stadium, home of the College World Series, and a poker game were all I knew about Omaha. I stumbled onto Omaha poker while flipping through television channels one day. It was a tournament featuring badly dressed men, fat men, and badly dressed fat men. They sat around a green table making bets and folding cards while I watched them in boredom from my couch. We returned to Hell Canyon and located Mitch.

"Make sure you get a receipt," he quipped.

With that we headed for Nebraska.

The landscape changed from desert to plains to grasslands, and I struggled to suppress a gnawing sense of unease. At last, we arrived in Omaha.

A restaurant had a sign that said 'Jimmy's Eggs'. Men and women ate bacon, eggs, and pancakes on brown tables. Their shoes sat on brown carpeting and their eyes looked at brown walls. Josephine glanced through a window. "He ordered the number three, most surprising." We turned onto another street and entered through the closed doors of the Czech and Slovak Educational Center and Cultural Museum, where the silhouettes of a man and a woman were waiting.

"Good afternoon, Josephine," the man said.

"Good afternoon, Roland. A pleasure to see you again,"

Josephine said.

Roland's silhouette stood tall and proud. "The heavens are magnificent as always, but inferior to your divine silhouette."

Josephine smiled. "Thank you for noticing."

Virgil said this. Can't the man get his own lines? I suppressed the urge to gag.

Roland smiled directly at me. "I see you've graced us with a beautiful jewel."

Josephine introduced us. "Her name is Dawn. Dawn this is Roland."

He took my hand and spoke with a smooth voice. "Pleased to meet you."

I pulled my hand back gave him a stiff reply. "Likewise." I knew his kind. Men with clever words but little substance. Virgil, now that's a man.

"Welcome to the Czech and Slovak Educational Center," the woman said. Her silhouette gave off a bruised light.

Josephine introduced us. "Dawn, this is Ester. She's going to help you." She said it in a way implying I was dumb.

Seeing the three of them look at me made me uncomfortable and Ester picked up on it.

"It's private. We'll talk about it tonight."

Josephine took her cue, gave me that dismissive 'daddy's money' gesture and left but Roland stayed to my dismay. He called out, in foreign words that made me squirm. "*Přijďte se setkat s novou dívkou.*" Silhouettes of men and women appeared. They were mostly of ivory, but there were some of bronze and others of copper. All of them had blue and green hues.

"Good afternoon everyone, this is Dawn, she'll be staying with us for a while," Ester said.

"Hi Dawn," they said in unison.

"Hi," I said defensively. I asked Roland what he just said.

"Come meet the new girl." He smiled.

Mitch's suggestion that I learn foreign languages came back and I needed to deal with this joker. "I'd like to learn this language."

"I'd be happy to teach you Czech." Roland's smile widened and to my dismay, his shade faded slightly.

Thankfully, Ester intervened. "I'll do that, Roland."

Norma and Patricia's warning about Josephine's friends flashed. "Is there someone who can also teach me French?" I still did not understand why Josephine's friends would be a threat but I would be prepared.

"You're in luck. I can teach you that too," she replied.

"You'd have more fun with Czech," Roland said.

I ignored him.

"Listen to the man," a man said.

"Yeah!" The rest of the silhouettes joined.

Ester waved them off. "She'll get to know you soon enough." She turned to give me a warm smile. "Let me show you around the museum."

Roland and the rest of the group left. There were exhibits of marionettes and intricately colored eggs. A banner saying 'CZ Choice of Champions' hung over some motorcycles. A plaque hung on a wall near the thermostat.

> 50,000 of these brave immigrants left the old country to make Nebraska their home.

"Do you like it?" she asked. I nodded. "It's too bad I can't introduce you to *kolach*. What I would give to get a bite of that wonderful fruit and cheese."

"What is *kolach*?" I remembered how the man from the Verde River missed beer.

"It's a pastry and I miss it so."

I wondered about the foods I loved.

"I miss lemon meringue pie."

"I miss that too."

A brief silence, then Ester said, "I grew up in the town of Lidice. The people call it the town of flowers. Lidice is located in what is now the Czech Republic but in my time, it was called Czechoslovakia."

I found her words reassuring. "I should go there and visit."

"Yes, but after you learn Czech."

I felt a smile form.

Ester's tone softened as she changed the subject. "It was probably an unpleasant surprise when you passed through."

It felt like she reached in and turned on my voice as my emotions gushed out with every word. A sensation of lightness filled my silhouette.

"Dawn, you're asking a question, which defies explanation, but meet me back here at sundown. I'll give you an answer that may be enough. In the meantime, check out the town."

"I'll be here."

I wandered the streets of Omaha and found myself in front of the Harry A Burke high school. Students passed around me and a girl wearing a violet helmet and a self-assured expression went by on a skateboard. Their lives looked so much easier. The trees showed green shoots and the sugar flowed inside just like Chlor-O-Phil said. Why did I refuse to cut him some slack?

I looked up to the sound of engines. A plane passed and the sunlight glanced off its silver exterior and vanished. An irritating voice interrupted me.

"Do you know you can overtake that plane?" Roland said.

My eyes narrowed and my silhouette flickered a red glow.

"Really?"

Roland's silhouette flickered purple before returning to a blue and green and his shade was light. "It's true. I'm not trying to make you look foolish."

I decided to keep him trapped in maybe. "Maybe later," I said.

"Have you seen the world from low-earth orbit?"

The flicker changed to an angry red and I used all my hostility to speak the next word.

"No!"

"Maybe you'll like to join me sometime. Seeing the lightning…" Roland stopped.

The hurt hit me hard as my silhouette bled purple. "Get out!"

Roland said he was sorry and left but the word left a deep cut. Desire for Virgil intruded as visions of him swooning over my French words danced in my head. My chest expanded as I pictured my French and my feminine conquering him so thoroughly he would be speaking my language. Then we would go to foreign lands where I could meet his connections and ditch my past.

A car horn reminded me I was in Omaha and Virgil liked Josephine.

***

Sunset eventually came and I rejoined Ester at the museum. "Let's go," she said.

We left Omaha and its city lights behind. Shortly, thereafter, we stopped in a fallow field. The moonless night put everything in pitch black except for the lights of a distant house and the occasional passing pickup truck.

"Repeat after me," Ester said. "Night, *noc, nuit.*"

Her command surprised me, but I complied.

"Welcome to your first lesson in Czech and French. Right now, the field is dirt, but they will plant the corn next month and come summer, it will be nice and tall."

She taught me more Czech and French words until the stars appeared.

"Do you see the stars, Dawn?"

The dirt gave off a pleasant odor. "Yes, I do."

Her voice became smoother and her glow shimmered in the darkness. "Do you know the stars and planets are linked?"

Her statement contradicted my eyes. "They're millions of light years apart."

"They're linked through Math."

I sensed she was leading up to something. "What does this have to do with me?"

"It has everything to do with you. Everything in the universe has Mathematical relationships, from the loveliest flower to a supernova. It's the fabric of creation built on formulas ranging from grade school arithmetic to the integrals of calculus. Math expresses itself in the languages of Chemistry, Physics, Engineering, Biology, Music, Literature, and Art." Her next sentence floored me. "It's also how you passed through."

"But I died of a lightning strike."

"The lightning bolt that killed you resulted from thousands of mathematical events. Unfortunately, you got the business end of the equations."

"I passed through because of equations?" My light flashed.

"Dawn, I understand that it's hard to accept but there's no good nor evil here, only accident."

My breath felt heavy. "An accident?"

"Life goes that way sometimes."

She was right but the fact was hard to take. All I could say was "why."

Ester didn't miss a beat. "I asked that same question at Mount Palomar to a man named Falco. Although my circumstances were different, I think his answer might apply here." She didn't wait for me to respond. "The only way to avoid accident is to have a math-free universe."

"A random equation killed me," I said.

"It's been like that for millions of years. Remember the dinosaurs?"

The light of a passing car went by and the lights in the house went dark. The tone of Ester's next words jolted me. "Are you going to mope in the dirt and complain how Math is a bitch or are you going to get off your ass and live? How are going to use your second chance, Dawn?"

Her challenge electrified me. The years I spent in the earthly life competing in 5K and 10K races roared back. How I hated it when someone passed me. Now the eternal life was on my shoulder and she was in my face. No moping for me. I got in her face and said the first thing that popped into my head.

"A fallow cornfield, you call this romance?"

Ester affected a deep voice. "I don't know what girls want. I'm trying."

A great weight released as we laughed. I thought about Hell Canyon and French words as we returned to the museum. She then threw me a curve.

"Why don't you give Roland a chance?"

"I met his kind in high school."

"He's not like that."

Memories of my funeral and Kyle rushed back. "Why don't

you take a chance on him, if he's so great?"

"I already have a man."

"Well, I want a man too. Someone like Virgil."

"Are you talking about Virgil, the Knight of Malta?"

"Who else?"

"The one who likes Josephine?"

Hesitation filled me. "Yes."

"Find another man."

My angry rose, but I kept it in check. "Why?"

"He's sweet on her. Look Dawn, other women have tried but he always goes back to Josephine."

I looked her square in the eye, gave her my best smile and smoothest voice. "Well, maybe a woman needs to speak Czech to the man." Ester shook her head as she smiled.

"I like your style but it isn't going to work. Besides, Roland is a better match for you."

Ester's comment flipped my color to red. Who was she to say what man I should have? "Him?"

Ester's head snapped back. "What's wrong with Roland?"

My teeth clamped shut. "Don't go there."

"Hey, don't be mad. Give him a chance."

"Drop it."

***

The kindness of others made the museum a haven. They patiently helped me as I spoke these new languages in broken words and sentences; Ester told me to keep at it and don't worry about mistakes. At first, I had to switch back to English but became more fluent by late April.

Seeing Ester was the leader, I decided it was in my best

interests to meet Roland, but I did it on my terms.

"OK, I'll meet him, but just this once."

"It's all I ask," she replied.

Roland and I met at the Harry A. Burke High School. The green shoots coming from the trees changed to leaves and flowers. Seeing the students flow in and out of the school gave me a good feeling. The skateboard girl and her whirring wheels and violet helmet arrived and rumbled down the sidewalk. I loved her self-assured expression.

A plane flew over the school on its way to an unknown city. Roland looked at me with eager anticipation.

"Let's go."

Were we really going to catch a plane? It would be like a dog catching a car. What would we do when got there? Roland had to be messing with me, but I did pass cars and trucks in Phoenix. We gave chase as the plane neared the horizon.

At first, nothing seemed to happen but soon I noticed the plane did not pull away. I kept pursuing, surprised that my body easily complied. The land below resembled little rectangles of varied brown shades. A narcotic sensation flooded me as the tail and rear engine came into sharp relief. The windows appeared and sunlight glinted off the fuselage.

"Here we are," Roland said. "Do you want a first class seat?"

We pulled up next to a window and looked in. How strange it was to look at the passengers from the outside. One was eating peanuts. What a surprise if he saw me. I smelled the mist as we passed through a cloud. We cruised with the plane for a while until the incessant engine noise annoyed me.

"Let's go inside."

The engine noise prevented him from hearing me, although he was only a couple feet away. I moved closer.

"Roland."

The plane entered a thick gray cloud. Suddenly, I didn't hear the engines.

"Roland?"

I had no idea which way was up or down as gray mist surrounded me. I chose a direction but the gray would not yield.

"Roland!"

It felt like I was trapped in a cotton ball as panic overtook me. My ears ached to hear the engines but only heard silence. A white streak followed by a crackle and boom, lightning. Intermittent streaks crackled and boomed past me as I rushed downward. I was about to scream when the gray parted and I emerged.

My butt was thirty-thousand feet in the air over a bunch of brown rectangles and the plane and Roland were nowhere to be found. The cloud was above me and I saw its edge. I rushed to it, found sunlight, and descended amid memories of the parking lot. The brown rectangles provided more details and a baseball field appeared as I got lower. Is this how Superman got started?

I landed next to an obelisk that said, 'Ramsey Serbousek Sports Complex, Dedicated 7-26-1980.' The outfield grass was in full green and fans wearing windbreakers sat in a shaded, freshly painted grandstand. Players played under a sky, looking like it was just washed. A team dressed in yellow shirts and blue pants were out on the diamond. The batter, dressed in a red shirt and gray pants, stood in the chalk-lined batter's box. I could make out a word HUSKIES written in cursive on the yellow shirts and BULLDOGS written in block on the batter's red shirt. The scoreboard showed the game had reached the top of the third inning and had words in whitewashed letters that said VISITORS, HOME, BALL, STRIKE, OUT, INNING and R-H-

E. A great white 'two' and 'three' stood to the right of VISITORS and HOME, respectively.

I moved from the obelisk to a chain-link fence that ran from the left field corner to behind home plate before making a right-angle turn to the right field corner. The infield with its pitcher's mound and bases looked the same as the ones I saw in Phoenix. Then just a few yards behind shortstop, I saw a black dot.

It looked like harmless speck taking in a game. I glanced at the wall of the third base dugout and saw an outline that had a darker shade. I stared at the wall and soon more outlines appeared. Who were they and why were they using their chameleon lights? More outlines appeared on the first base dugout roof and the right field foul pole. One of them approached me.

"*Espèce d'idiot, que faites-vous?*" he yelled.

Surprised by his French, I looked at him blankly.

He changed to English. "You idiot, what are you doing?"

"What do you mean, what am I doing?"

"Change to the chameleon light!"

I tried, but it flickered like a poor cigarette lighter.

"Do it!"

"I'm new at this!"

A "pling" sound from the aluminum bat distracted me. I followed the ball's rise into the air and as the ball descended, I could see the shortstop pass the speck as he ran backwards into left field. Out of the corner of my eye, the outlines I saw just a few seconds earlier changed into silhouettes and closed in on the speck like a flash flood. Just as the man tried to block my view, I heard a horrific scream.

"Never mind, they got him." He let me see again.

"Who did they get?"

"Giles Ferrer."

Josephine's silhouette appeared and Norma and Patricia's warning blared. *She has a lot of French friends so be careful what you do and say.*

The batter reached third base. The baseball lay in the grass like an Easter egg next to the sprawled shortstop and left fielder. Another player retrieved the ball and threw it to the catcher standing at home plate. The scream repeated itself.

Josephine's group gave off a red and yellow hue, resembling a horde of wasps. The man rushed toward the group while I followed, but slowed down when the screaming intensified. I arrived to see Josephine inside the black hole and say, *"Bon matin, Giles, maintenant, vous allez découvrir comment la lumière brûlures!"*

I asked the man who blocked my view to translate.

She said, "Good Morning Giles. Time to find how light burns."

Josephine's red and yellow glow intensified as I watched Giles Ferrer wither and curl. It reminded me of second grade when I trained the summer sunlight through a magnifying glass onto a leaf. Even now, I remembered the unique intense heat and the effect it had on my hand when I made the mistake of putting it behind the glass.

"Stop it!" I yelled.

The raging crowd absorbed my command.

"Stop it, damn you," I shouted.

"Why are you telling her to stop?" the man asked.

"What do you mean why am I telling her to stop? She's hurting him."

The man's colors deepened. "It's nothing like the hurting he inflicted on us."

"Stop it," I yelled again.

"Shut up," the man yelled back.

That's when I remembered Dad telling me I had no right to add to a man's suffering and that Christians do not wish suffering on others.

A Frenchman replaced Josephine as Ferrer's agony continued. A woman replaced the Frenchman, and they continued the ritual until satisfied. Giles laid there, his black exterior blistered, and the game played on.

"What you're doing to this man is evil." Aware that I was taking on a crowd, I felt my stomach flutter.

"You should shut up," came a voice.

"Yeah," more voices joined.

Josephine's smooth voice parted the air. "*Arrêtez s'il vous plaît, je peux gérer sa saveur.*" The crowd laughed but Josephine silenced them with the raise of her hand as she squared herself to me.

"Do you appreciate that you're operating from a position of ignorance?" she asked.

My anger pushed back against the flutter and I was about to respond, when Josephine continued.

"You see but do not know. You're like the flower children at a wedding. The marriage takes place, but they do not appreciate what marriage is. Likewise, with this man, you understand nothing." The crowd laughed, but again she waved them off.

"You have no right to add to his suffering. It's enough he's condemned to run from nature." I guess I wasn't funny because the crowd didn't laugh.

Josephine showed a razor smile. "Why don't you ask Giles what he did?"

Giles' body now resembled a bowl of rotten fruit as hideous

glows of yellow, brown, and black made him hard to look at. "Why is he changing color?" I asked.

Someone in the mob shouted. "That's the bacteria and the fungi. They're so small we can only observe their effects."

Josephine smiled when I said, "Everything comes to the eternal life." I approached Giles, who mixed his screams with crying.

"You need to back away unless you want to burn him too," Josephine said.

"Keep him burning," a voice yelled from the crowd.

I backed away slightly and, unsure if he spoke English, asked, "Are you Giles Ferrer?"

"I just wanted to see my great grandson play baseball," he said. The bacteria and fungi deepened their colors and the odor moved me back a step.

"How did you attract so much vengeance?" I asked.

"Too bad his great grandson couldn't make the catch. He will have a nasty headache," Josephine crowed.

The crowd laughed.

"What did you do?" I asked but Giles did not answer.

"I'll tell you what he did," Josephine said. Her red and yellow deepened. "Do you know what this white mustached and dirty mouthed traitor did? He gave a woman an ultimatum: Perform sexual favors or watch her brother put on the occupier's train. She didn't do that. Then the next week he repeated his ultimatum. She refused again, and he put her mother on the train. She refused again the next week, and he put her father on the train. She's still looking for them." Josephine pointed to the pack. "Look at the people out there. They're still looking for their families and friends. The eternal life is a large place and it took us a long time to track him down, but today we got him. So don't tell us about evil."

"Is it true what she said?"

Josephine advanced. "Tell her what kind of train it was."

"Yes, it's true," Giles said.

"Tell her what kind of train it was," Josephine shouted.

Giles didn't respond.

Josephine pounced on him. "Tell her."

Giles screamed his response. "The train was to send Jews and others to Dachau and other camps."

Josephine said, "*Tu n'aimes pas les filles ou suis-je trop femme pour toi*" before getting off him. Giles screamed some more and the crowd laughed.

I struggled to absorb what I heard. "Why would you do such a thing to one of your fellow countrymen?"

"Because she was pretty and I had to have her."

The magnitude of his response shocked me.

Josephine gave me a smug look. "You came from a nice better homes and garden family. While you worried about your grades and pimples, we worried about the persecutors who came for us. But today, the man who violated others received the violence of light."

The mob mirrored Josephine's smug look as I understood why she held me in such low regard. I sensed them watching me as the scoreboard showed the game was in the bottom of the sixth inning. I took pity on Giles as the bacteria and fungi continued to mutilate him. He may have been a robber of sex and life, but meting out such cruelty was not justice. I chose the next words as best I could.

"You had no business adding to his punishment."

"Don't tell me what my business is," Josephine replied. I was sure if she had a stinger, she would have used it.

My stomach fluttered again. "I'll tell you what your business is and you're going to listen."

"We're done here." With a wave of her hand, Josephine signaled the crowd.

A voice from behind surprised me. "Yes, you are." It was Roland.

Chapter 7

I turned my eyes away as Roland's silhouette displayed a white hue.

Josephine's voice displayed a respectful tone. "Good afternoon, Roland. We were just leaving."

I should have kept my mouth shut. "He came to watch his great grandson play baseball. You couldn't even give him that?"

"The crocodiles nurture their own flesh and blood too," Josephine said.

"Dawn, back off," Roland said.

I did so.

"I hope you meet the woman he did this to. Don't lecture me until you talk to her." Josephine and her companions left.

"Roland, why did your color turn white?" I asked.

Roland's blue and green color returned, but the white flickered. He gave off an embarrassed smile. "It means courage."

The bacteria and fungi's disgusting colors made me pity Giles. Maybe he was a Nazi collaborator, but he didn't merit such cruelty. Unable to cure his wounds, I gave him some dignity.

"Hey, Giles, which boy was your great grandson?"

Giles replied with a firm voice. "The shortstop."

"Would you tell me more about him?" I asked.

"He's such a magnificent boy. I'm so proud of him."

Giles' great grandson was Joseph Martin. The words spilled out from Giles about Joseph's life. He had good grades, which gave him an excellent chance to receive a scholarship. His defensive skills at shortstop attracted college scouts from the community colleges. Billy Palmer was his best friend. As he kept speaking, I realized I was the first person he met in a long time who showed an interest in his life. Dad's statement that Christians do not wish suffering on others now made sense, but Josephine's statement that crocodiles nurture their own flesh and blood was also true. Then Giles made a surprising statement.

"At least Josephine gave me a second chance."

"She just fed you to bacteria and fungi."

Giles gave a small smile. "I don't have to run any more." He then told me what Hell was like.

Giles lived his eternal life, hiding in rock crevices and keeping his eyes and head moving for any animal or human silhouette. Touching a plant would scorch him and he could only come out on moonless nights lest the moonlight betray his position. He lived in constant loneliness and fear of ambush. Even a casual chat with a fellow black hole was dangerous. However, no man can hold off loneliness forever, and Giles was no exception. His need to see Joseph play led to his end.

The bacteria and fungi continued their work, and the rotten colors deepened as the minutes passed. Giles winced, but did not scream as I watched him shrink.

"Giles, you're getting smaller."

"They're eating my darkness," Giles said. "Soon, I will disappear."

The thought of him vanishing unnerved me. "Maybe there's some light in you."

"I did enough bad things to snuff out my light."

With that statement, and his pitiful state, I gave him a blessing, even though he probably didn't deserve it.

"Peace be with you."

Sadness overwhelmed me as Roland and I watched Giles disappear. This man had parents who had high hopes for him on his birth day. Now he died all over again on a lonely field seen from the sky as a brown patch. I asked him a question to distract me.

"What town is this?"

"Would it matter if I said Ainsworth, or Pender, or Atkinson?"

The question seemed stupid, given his circumstances.

"I'm sorry about the plane. Pilots rarely fly into thunderstorms," Roland said.

The man looked for me and defended me, yet showed humility. I recalled Josephine's respectful tone.

"She seems to respect you."

"We did war service together."

His response staggered me. "You and Josephine were in Iraq?"

He gave a rueful smile. "Yes, we were."

He talked briefly about his life as a searcher and how it soon ended after Iraq. "We weren't the same afterwards. Josephine went on, but I couldn't do it any more."

The look in his face told me to back off. I asked him about her followers. "Why do the Frenchmen and Frenchwomen follow her? They think she's some sort of saint?"

"She helped get their country back."

I made a sarcastic reply. "I bet she got two funerals too."

"She did." He then showed me the magnitude of my ignorance.

Roland told about Josephine's exploits just before and during World War II. She volunteered to serve France without thinking twice about it, took significant risks to gather intelligence before the war started, and helped form the resistance after the Germans occupied France. Finally, he told about the medals the French government awarded her after the war, the Medal of the Resistance with Rosette and the Chevalier of the Legion of Honor.

He showed me she was more than a wartime heroine. One day she entertained in Venezuela and found a child in squalor. Naked – she clothed him, hungry – she fed him, homeless – she sheltered him, orphaned – she adopted him.

I passed through and she found me. Roland agreed Josephine was not a saint because saints perform miracles, but he made me concede she performed miracle-like things. Roland told how the citizens of Paris attended Josephine's first funeral, where she received full military honors, the only American to receive such tribute. He then told me about Josephine's second funeral, which was in Monaco, where Princess Grace took care of the arrangements. Suddenly, he surprised me.

"I'm glad I found you, Dawn."

"I'm glad you found me too."

"Dawn, you have a dazzling light and a big heart and I would like to be near it more." His hand reached out and touched me.

A sensation of someone walking around inside me and opening the drawers to my secrets overran me. His touch was not brutish and blunt, but gentle as his masculine heat filled me. My silhouette wobbled as Ester's words roared through my head. Fear intervened to protect my secrets as Roland's hand moved, but passion fought to keep his touch.

Fear and passion compromised as Roland leaned in and kissed me. Passion could go wherever it chose as long as it did not open fear's secrets.

My shade vanished and my color changed to pink as I gave

him some of me.

Ester saw us holding hands when we returned to Omaha.

"I guess the two of you had a good time," she said.

We told Ester we chased an airplane and got caught in a thundercloud. Suddenly, I remembered Josephine said something in French, which I did not understand.

"Hey Ester, what does *Arrêtez s'il vous plaît, je peux gérer sa saveur mean?*"

"It means, 'stop please, I can handle her flavor.' Where did you hear that?"

"She tangled with Josephine," Roland said.

Red erupted from my silhouette. "That bitch has disrespected me for the last time." Ester laughed.

"That's why you must learn foreign languages."

I intended to speak French like a Marseilles woman.

Summer came and classes at Harry A. Burke ended. Fields that were dirt in March changed to corn in June. Hot mornings followed by late afternoon rains swept through Omaha and pitter-pattered off the museum's roof. My Czech and French were as good as my English and I could move between them as easily as a race car driver shifts gears. Virgil, Josephine, Mitch, and Hell Canyon were distant memories. I had friends, and Roland made me feel like the luckiest woman in the world. He was from Madison, Wisconsin, and he had two sisters. His parents were college professors who taught history and engineering. I told him my parents owned an insurance franchise as I carefully screened my past.

I recalled that first night when Ester told me why I passed. Suddenly, I recalled her saying her circumstances were different. I was about to seek her when she came by.

"Hey Ester, before you explained to me why I had to pass

through, you said your circumstances were different. Could you explain?"

Ester gazed at me and said, "A Russian soldier killed me." A smile slowly formed, and her blue and green color shimmered. "I guess you now know how I got my bruised light."

Ester passed through on 22 August 1968, which was her eighteenth birthday.

She was in Prague, not too far from Wenceslas Square, when the Russians streamed into Czechoslovakia with tanks and guns. "We thought we could beat the Russians and keep the Prague Spring going by spray painting the street signs, except I got more of the paint on me." She let out a smile. "We tried to kill them with confusion." She recounted the horror of Russian trucks and infantry bearing down on her, ordering her to stop. Instead, she ran, and the soldiers pursued. A squeal of tires and she looked back to see a truck hit some of them. Ester turned into an alley, only to find a dead end.

"Red paint covered my palms, and the soldiers stopped within a few meters. One of them aimed his rifle, and I swore I could see the bullet when I looked down into that hole. I was about to laugh and say 'Looks like you caught me red-handed' but I shouted in Russian, 'live free or die.'"

The soldier released his bullet, which wrecked her pretty face and ended the Prague Spring.

Live free or die. Ester's statement struck me as odd. "That's New Hampshire's state motto. How did you know that?"

"I saw it on the cars' license plates when the Communists televised America's Presidential primaries."

Ester gave me a playful look. "Have you ever looked down the barrel of a gun?"

My silhouette wobbled as I shook my head.

"I don't recommend it." Ester gave a wry smile. "I made a lot of mistakes when I was seventeen but the one that killed me was thinking I could bring America to my parents."

I held back tears. "What happened after you passed through?"

"A kind, soft-spoken searcher named Sylvia found and took me to America. It was strange to cross the Atlantic Ocean without an airplane or a ship."

It amazed me she was so trusting.

Upon arriving in America, Sylvia took Ester to Mount Palomar, which is in California. Ester said the fragrant juniper trees and pine made her feel good. They arrived at an observatory and a silhouette of a man named Falco greeted them at the A. W. Greenway Visitor Center. He gave her a tour of the observatory and its thick beams, naked walls, orange lights, dim interior, and musty scent.

"He told me I also choose equations the universe uses."

I gave her a blank look. But Ester was patient.

"Falco explained the soldier had a choice between two equations, arrest or shooting. Unfortunately, he shot."

Ester continued. "Falco asked if I would use my second chance to release equations of love or equations of hate. I do my best to choose love. That's your choice too, Dawn."

Sympathy for Ester filled me. "At least that soldier's a black hole."

"Actually, he's my boyfriend."

I had a sensation of falling through a trapdoor. I checked Ester's face to see if she was joking, but she was serious. "What?"

Ester's light intensified. "His name is Ivan and I'm so fortunate."

Confusion and anger swirled. "What do you mean, you're so fortunate? He killed you."

"Yes, that was unfortunate, but it's all good now."

I could not grasp how this admirable woman could allow such a thing. "I didn't expect you, of all people, to be a battered girlfriend."

Ester's rage instantly flashed a beet red. "You shut your mouth. You know nothing about Ivan or his circumstances. He gave me in the eternal life what I lacked in the earthly life and never think I would let anybody hit me."

I knew I was wrong and did my best to atone. "Okay, I went too far with that statement but I cannot understand why your boyfriend is the man who ended your earthly life by putting a bullet in your face."

The hurt look on Ester's face showed my words stung. But she replied calmly. "Let me tell you about Ivan. He searched for me after he passed through to explain why he killed me. I wanted nothing to do with him or any Russian, but Falco challenged me to give him a chance to make it right."

Ester told Ivan's story. He was an eighteen-year-old soldier in the Russian army. He had only been a soldier for six months when he and his fellow soldiers received orders to quell a 'disturbance' in Czechoslovakia.

Ivan said that underneath all the joking and tough talk, they were scared kids when they boarded the transport plane for Prague and seeing his sergeant's grim face didn't help. Sergeant Petrovich was his name and Ivan would find out much later why he was grim. He saw combat there in 1948.

Ivan said his uniform felt like a bullseye when they arrived at the airbase and got off the plane. Ears and eyes scanned everything, but all was quiet. An olive green convoy truck with a red star on the door pulled up and Sergeant Petrovich ordered them in. Ivan remembered the smell of the tires. The driver put the truck in gear and joined a convoy of trucks as they left.

Ivan's stomach was in knots as they entered Prague. Angry citizens waving red, white, and blue Czechoslovak flags shouted at them. Their colorful clothes stood in stark contrast to the soldiers' green uniforms and red stars. Ivan sensed they perceived him and his fellow soldiers as an infection, and he had to steady his hand to insert the cartridge when Sergeant Petrovich ordered them to load their rifles. The soldiers made eye contact with each other and communicated in unspoken words the fundamental command: Protect each other.

The August sun beat down, and the convoy became lost when they encountered the spray painted street signs. The trucks ground to a stop and everyone became worried about snipers concealed among the angry crowd. To everyone's relief, Sergeant Petrovich ordered the driver to take a side street.

The street was empty. The truck made two turns and soon joined another convoy of trucks. Ivan was just starting to relax when the tires squealed, jerking him forward, followed by a 'whump' and a sudden stop.

"Get the girl," Sergeant Petrovich yelled. Ivan and his fellow soldiers jumped out of the truck and saw two soldiers writhing on the pavement and a girl running up the street.

He was in the lead, but could hear the breathing of two soldiers behind him. He remembered to switch the safety off his rifle as the woman turned into an alley. Ivan turned hard and stopped when he saw her trapped. He raised his rifle as she slowly turned.

He could not tell if she had a grenade. Before he commanded her to step toward him, she said, "live free or die." He fired the bullet and wrecked her pretty face.

Sergeant Petrovich came up and plodded to the fallen woman. His face grimaced for an instant as he gazed at her. He turned to Private Ivan Sokolov and, for a moment, looked at him like he shot his daughter before his grim face returned. "I didn't order you to shoot," he said.

Ivan developed a drinking problem after that, which eventually killed him.

Ester stopped for a moment and looked right in my eyes. "I passed through quickly, and he passed through slowly." She then challenged me.

"Do you think Ivan and I should be eternal enemies?"

I shook my head. Forgive him, yes, but love him? It was like dividing by zero. "It's messed up."

I told Roland what happened.

"What's your problem, Dawn? They gave each other a second chance."

"But he took away her first chance."

He repeated Ester's challenge. "Do you want them to remain eternal enemies?" I had to concede I didn't.

"No, Roland, I don't want that."

***

The blistering July sun came to the practice field at Harry A. Burke high school. Football players wearing helmets, t-shirts, and shorts drilled to the stop and start commands of a coach's whistle. Ester approached and confronted me with a grim look and grim colors.

"You're not being straight with Roland."

My head snapped back. "What do you mean, I'm not being

straight with Roland? He knows everything about me."

"Dawn, that's not true."

She was on to me, but how? I went on offense and affected a red color. "Don't insult me."

"The people here Dawn are pretty open about their past, but you ration what you say."

I threw more rage at her. "Everybody knows what they need to know about me. The rest of it is private." I added to my sentence on the spur of the moment. "Only for Roland."

Ester showed a restrained red. "Okay, I'll let it go if you're being true to Roland, but remember this. You may fool him, but you can't fool me." She then left.

I sensed she would not quit until she found out who I was. Leaving Omaha was the only way to protect my secret, but that would mean losing Roland. However, I came up with a solution: He would come with me.

I found Roland at the museum.

"Hey Roland, let's get out of Omaha and travel the world."

"That's sounds like fun."

It was easier than I thought." I would like to see Paris."

"I want to go to Hell Canyon first. Then, we'll go wherever you like."

A feeling of worry intruded. "Why do you want to go there? It's just a terminal."

"I want to thank the people who brought you to me."

I quickly assessed the risk. Refusing to go would make Roland suspicious, but I couldn't stay in Omaha because Ester was already suspicious. Hell Canyon was my only choice.

"All right, we'll go," I said.

"It probably won't take that long. Meet some people, make some small talk, and leave."

I focused on leaving.

Hell Canyon looked the same to me, but Roland looked like a little kid who woke up to see lots of Christmas presents. He saw Josephine and waved to her, and she waved back.

"I'm going to talk to her."

I concealed my displeasure. "Okay."

I saw Norma and Patricia under a cottonwood tree. Patricia's glow was purple, and she was crying while Norma's hue was blue and green. I joined them when Norma waved to me.

"Why is Patricia weeping?" I asked.

Norma replied with a twinkle in her eye. "Patricia let Mitch build up her heart."

I finished her sentence. "Only to destroy it utterly and completely."

"You got it."

"He was so much, man," Patricia said.

"Oh, Trish, you're so melodramatic," Norma replied.

Patricia continued crying, and Norma seemed to enjoy herself. "Trish, when are you going to learn nothing is forever in the eternal life?"

Patricia did not respond. Norma turned to me and said, "There's a cure for this but unfortunately it's not available."

I sensed this happened before. "What's that?"

Norma stifled a laugh. "It's the black, brown, and white treatment."

"The what?"

"It's a half gallon each of chocolate and vanilla ice cream mixed with a half bottle of whiskey." Norma changed her voice." Warning: Side effects include brain freeze, nausea, and a hangover. Do not use black, brown, and white if you are already with a man as it may lead to shameful behavior." Norma laughed.

Patricia interrupted me before I could reply. "I'm giving up men."

"But you like squeezing bananas," Norma replied.

Patricia's purple hue changed to red. "Dammit, Norma, why are you so crude?"

"Well, I dated an accountant named Doug, who taught me all the dirty words." Norma got near Patricia and said, "Hey there, cowboy…"

"That will not work this time," Patricia replied.

Norma persisted. "Come on say, 'Hey there cowboy'."

"I'm serious I'm giving up men."

"I will not quit until you say 'hey there, cowboy.'"

Patricia's silhouette flickered red for an instant. "I'm serious."

"Come on. Hey there, cowboy…" Norma's voice stretched the word cowboy.

Patricia pouted. "Okay, Okay, hey there cowboy."

"Say it with some feeling."

Patricia gritted her teeth. "Hey there cowboy."

"Again."

"Hey there cowboy."

"One more time."

They said it together, repeating the words. "Hey there, cowboy. Hey there, cowboy. Hey there cowboy." It sounded like a cheer at a sporting event. Without warning, they abruptly completed the sentence.

"Hey there, cowboy, with the big bandana. Let me tug on your red banana."

Patricia's purple vanished as they giggled. "Norma, you know how to make me laugh."

"Who else is going to help me destroy hearts utterly and

completely?"

"Okay, maybe I can give men one more chance."

"Good, because it would have been a sad day for mankind if you retired your banana squeezer."

Patricia let out a small smile. "Well, it is high performance and there are so many ripe bananas."

"The harvest is plenty and the laborers are few."

They laughed, and I left before my face changed color.

Roland was talking to Josephine.

"Virgil gets one date with you, but there's a catch. He cannot pursue you any more if you do not want a second date."

She looked at the trees and then at Roland. "So you're saying I should give him a date where he recites his poems but after that he must leave me alone."

"You make the rules for him."

The seconds passed, and I forced myself not to fidget as I watched. At last, she replied.

"Okay, it looks like it will work, but I need you to find me the most inopportune location."

Roland smiled. "Okay, that shouldn't be too hard."

"I'll tell Virgil. By the way, there's a nice girl I think you should meet," Josephine replied as she left.

"But I have a girlfriend."

"You can do better."

Roland smiled as I approached, but his smile vanished when he saw my angry colors.

"What did you just do?" I asked.

"I just solved Josephine's problem with Virgil. She's going to give him one date and one date only. She wants me to pick a place for them if he agrees."

I could feel the heat of my red glow radiate from silhouette.

"We came to Hell Canyon to play matchmaker?"

"I'm sorry, Dawn. I should've asked you first." My thoughts advised me that anger might complicate my plans to leave. I made sure my next words were sweet and conciliatory.

"Okay, we'll do this because you gave her your word, but I want to see Paris."

"Agreed."

Josephine returned with a triumphant smile. "Virgil has agreed to my terms. Now Roland, I need you to find the most drab and nondescript location you can find."

Roland squeezed my hand. "Okay, *we* can do that."

Josephine looked at me dismissively. "All right, she might be of use, but I don't see how."

"Hey don't treat her that way. She's got courage."

His statement surprised both of us. "Really, how so?" Josephine asked.

"She stood up to you and your French friends."

Josephine laughed. "That's not courage. That's stupidity."

"Call it whatever you like, but treat her right. By the way, what are the terms?"

The terms required Virgil to recite two poems, plus his own poem in the middle of the afternoon at a drab and nondescript location. In addition, he was to answer what she missed most about the earthly life and he could not request a second date. Roland surprised us again.

"We're going to amend this agreement, Josephine."

"No, we're not."

"Yes, we are, and this is what you're going to do. You're going to be nice to Dawn after your date with Virgil. Otherwise, we will not be friends for a while."

Josephine glared at me and gave Roland a hard look. Roland

pressed her.

"Do you want me to help you or do you want to do it yourself?"

Josephine gave a respectful smile. "Roland, I've got to admit you know how to negotiate. I'll do it your way." She left and avoided looking at me.

My heart pounded with admiration for Roland, but I was not letting up. "I did not pass through to the eternal life to get a mother-in-law."

"I'll make sure she keeps her word. Then we go to Paris."

Visions of the Eiffel Tower danced in my head, and soon I would ditch my past.

Chapter 8

Finding a drab, nondescript, and undesirable spot was harder than we thought as the harsh Southwestern desert has a beauty all its own. Southern California has Joshua trees and rock escarpments and Arizona has awe-inspiring horizons. It wasn't until Roland and I went to the Navajo Tribal Reservation where we found what I needed.

Milepost thirty-eight stood next to a four-lane road in a desert that was sufficiently drab and nondescript. The pale green grasses and tan bushes looked like they needed weeding. The dull gray rocks and brown sand tired the eye. A solitary off-white boulder with the word 'TONI' in faded red paint sat on a nearby hill and a heart hung over the 'I' like a partially deflated valentine. A white sign, which said '491 New Mexico,' twisted in the wind. No other landmarks marked the location, and the air did not give the faintest scent of moisture.

Josephine had the look of a woman sitting in a dentist's chair as the partially deflated valentine overlooked the blacktop highway behind her. Virgil had the hopeful look of a man hoping decades of effort would pay off, and seeing him made the warm rush return. Nobody said anything as we waited for the sun to reach mid-afternoon. I smiled and made small talk.

"Virgil, will you tell us what poems you plan to recite to the lady?"

Josephine snickered.

"Are you snickering because I referred to you as a lady?"

Verbally cutting her never felt so good.

"Shut up and get on with it," Josephine snarled.

"Back it off, Dawn," Roland said.

Virgil interrupted us before we could fight, and his confidence emerged to compete with the hopeful look. "My pleasure. First, I will recite three sonnets from Shakespeare and then a poem I composed."

She's rejecting a man who recites poems. What an idiot.

Josephine interrupted him. "You will only recite two sonnets plus your poem."

Virgil's cool, certain voice asserted itself and made my stomach flutter. "I accept the lady's terms."

Roland reminded Virgil of another rule. "Virgil, do you understand you cannot see her again if that's her desire?"

"She's worth the chance, small as it may be." Again, his certain voice made my stomach flutter while Josephine shifted slightly.

Roland made the final announcement when the sunlight hit the rock square. "Mid-afternoon is here. Dawn and I will leave you two alone."

"Thank you," Virgil said. Josephine looked at me as if I stole her purse.

"Thank you for granting me an audience," he said.

"You are welcome." Her face was a perfectly blank slate of indifference.

We went past the rock when Roland took my hand and said, "Let's see what happens."

"Why?"

"He's been trying to get this chance for forty years."

I reluctantly consented.

Virgil announced the program, his voice smooth and refined.

"The program comprises two sonnets from William Shakespeare: Sonnets 23 and 26. I will conclude with my composition titled *The Butterfly and the Rock.*"

"Please proceed." Her face remained impassive.

"Sonnet 23," he pronounced.

As an unperfect actor on the stage,
Who with his fear is put besides his part,
Or some fierce thing replete with too much rage,
Whose strength's abundance weakens his own heart,
So I, for fear of trust, forge to say
The perfect ceremony of love's [rite],
And in mine own love's strength seem to decay,
O'ercharged with burthen of mine own love's might.
O, let my books then be then the eloquence
And dumb presagers of my speaking breast,
Who plead for love, and look for recompense,
More than that tongue that more hath more express'd.
O, learn to read what silent love has writ:
To hear with eyes belongs to love's fine wit.

Oh Virgil, how can you not know that you waste poetry on that hog?

He twitched when she did not respond and proceeded to the next sonnet.

Lord of my love, to whom in vassalage
Thy merit hath my duty strongly knit,
To thee I send this written ambassage
To witness duty, not to show my wit;
Duty so great, which wit so poor as mine
May make seem bare, in wanting words to show it,
But that I hope some good conceit of thine
In thy soul's thought (all naked) will bestow it;

Till whatsoever star that guides my moving
Points on me graciously with fair aspect,
And puts apparel on my tottered loving,
To show me worthy of thy sweet respect:
Them may I dare to boast how I do love thee,
Till then, not show my head where thou mayst prove me.

Virgil's face showed he was down to his last chance as she remained impassive. I felt sorry for him, as defeat was just a poem away.

"As you wish, I will not recite Sonnet 57. Instead, I will recite my final composition, *The Butterfly and the Rock*, which I composed for you."

Josephine's face remained unmoved. *How can she be so callous?* A joke crept in. You can take a whore to culture, but you can't make her think.

I am the stone of Malta land
I keep the sand and grass bound in one tight band
I keep the ground for man and beast firm
Through day and night, when each takes turn
I see flowers by day and stars by night
The winds come and go, but it's still the same sight
Spring returned to Malta land
The breeze was gentle, the flowers fanned
When I saw fluttering in the air
A butterfly of orange and black wing so fair
It had no worry. It had no care.
It flitted from flower to flower, there and there
Oh, such heavenly delight
To join that butterfly in divine flight
But it was not for me to leave Malta land

Fated to keep sand and grass bound in one tight band
Oh, butterfly of such delicate lace
Come here and rest upon my stony face
But the butterfly seemed not to care
Flitting from flower to flower there to there
Such beauty ached my sight
All I had was day and night
Please, butterfly of such delicate lace
Come rest upon my stony face.
But the butterfly seemed not to care
Dancing from flower to flower, there and there
Please take pity on this rock of Malta land
Fated to keep sand and grass bound in one tight band
Please, I know I have a stony face
Please come here and give me grace
The butterfly seemed to leave me to my grief
But no, it circled to me like lazy leaf
Landing on my face of stony gray
Wings spread out in full array

Virgil bowed. "Thank you, Miss Josephine, for giving me an audience. I hope to have earned the right to grace your stage a second time."

Josephine's impassive face softened. "Men have offered me many things. The finest gems, so I could be glamorous. Wealth so I could have whatever I desired. Business deals so I could have influence. Dance so I could have style and grace. Sex so I could be feminine."

She showed him her eyes. "However, you were the first man to offer me poetry so I could have beauty, humility, and respect."

For a moment, Virgil seemed confused. Finally, he broke the

silence, and said with strength and humility, "Let's talk."

Her face softened some more. "What about?"

"What did you like about La Créole?"

Her face brightened. "That operetta, it's been a long time since anyone asked me about it."

I wanted to leave. "Roland, let's go."

Roland was unmoved. "I want to see how this turns out."

A cloud of frustration enveloped me as I sulked. Then, I saw the silhouettes of Mitch, Norma, Patricia, and some others.

I tapped Roland's shoulder and pointed at Mitch. "Roland, how do they know?"

"It's hard to keep a secret at Hell Canyon."

Josephine went on about how she gave the operetta life, how it advanced her career and led to the restaurant business. It was like listening to an old woman talking about boring stories of her glory days, but Virgil watched her closely. "They found out I was more than a banana dancer."

"You were amazing as Dora. Can you sing me a verse?" Virgil asked.

"It's been so long." She smiled and reveled in his request, pretending to be reluctant.

"Can you just try it?" Virgil prodded.

"I forgot most of the words and it has been a long time since I sang."

"Please."

"Well, OK."

Si vous croyez que ca ma muse
Vous a vez l'air toute' ba hi
Vous a vez la mine con fuse
D'un'rosier devant le bail li

She stumbled through the verse and her voice had some rust, but we did not come to judge her talent. She changed the conversation.

"OK, Virgil, how did you come to know Shakespeare?"

Virgil's face lit up. "Back in the day, a friend of mine and his girlfriend took me to the Globe Theater, where the Bard would have an actor recite some sonnets during the intermission. Too bad the Theater burned down."

My mouth dropped as I stared at him.

"The play was Macbeth. I had little background in Art at the time and I admit I'm still limited today, but I knew this play was special."

Virgil talked more about the Globe Theater, but would stop occasionally and ask Josephine if she wanted to know more. He had such class, such pearls, and yet wasted on such swine. I hung on every word.

The lowering sun poured color and shadow into the landscape, deepening the hue of the rocks and sand. I looked up and saw the boulder had a stronger tone of white, and even the red paint of TONI looked bolder. The two talked about other things as darkness arrived with a full moon that provided a dim light.

"You know who I would like to see again?" Virgil asked.

"No, who?" Josephine replied.

"Matthew, he was the man who found me when I passed through. I haven't seen him in years."

"Sylvia was the woman who found me," Josephine replied.

"You never forget the one who found you," Virgil said.

Those words etched Josephine's memory into my thoughts.

"Do you want to hear a secret?" Virgil asked with a smile.

"I would love to." Josephine had the look of a little girl about to receive her favorite dessert.

"During the battle of Malta, I had to leave my post to use the privy. While I was relieving myself, some Turk thought it would be funny to launch a cannonball my way."

"Oh, no!"

"I could hear the breeze from the cannonball as it passed my ear. Plaster and wood covered me. It definitely ruined the moment."

She laughed.

"My friends told privy jokes for two days at my expense, saying things like 'Don't get caught with your pants down when you go to Heaven' among other rude things."

She laughed some more. "Oh Virgil, that's priceless." They laughed together and then she declared, "Let me tell you a secret I've told no one."

"I'm listening." Virgil drew close.

"It was 1939, and I was at the Italian embassy. I had an envelope pinned inside my underwear that described Germany's planned supply and troop movements. I was heading to the woman's room to pass the envelope to my contact when a German officer stopped me and insisted we dance. As we danced, the envelope shifted and started rubbing me in the wrong place. I knew the stationery was rough, but now it felt like sandpaper."

"Ow! That sounds most unpleasant."

"It was. Do you know how hard it is to smile when you're rubbed the wrong way?"

Virgil laughed first, with Josephine following.

Josephine kept laughing as she said, "That envelope kept rubbing every time we turned. Finally, the music stopped, and I rushed to the woman's room with a wide, fast stride."

Josephine caught enough of her breath to continue. "It

seemed like I sat in that stall for hours. Fortunately, the bathroom had some lotion, so I could get some relief." They continued giggling until it finally faded in the moonlight.

"Later on, the French government gave you a uniform and the rank of sub-lieutenant."

"Yes, and they gave me medals too, their highest honors."

"Were you proud to wear the uniform?"

"Very!"

"It's what you miss most about the earthly life," Virgil said, and then he kissed her.

The kiss paralyzed Josephine's face with surprise. Josephine shuddered as he kissed her again and said, "I knew you were something special when you danced, just like Macbeth."

"He did it!" Roland exclaimed.

Josephine moved away slightly, showing her shade vanished. The silhouetted nipples spread across her breasts like dark roses in bloom, and a hot pink glow covered her. Her eyes were her last line of defense as she kept her legs closed. Her shaking mouth stuttered. "I do not see how…."

Virgil's masculine face knew he caught her. He lost his shade and his glow changed to a reddish-orange as a red-hot line protruded from between his hips. Virgil cut off her sentence and put new words in her ears. "You are the name." Josephine's legs parted, her color deepened, and she cried with intensity. We needed to leave.

"Roland, let's get out of here."

Roland's eyes were wide open. I hit him upside the head.

"Roland, really?"

Roland put his face on his shoulder. "Oops, sorry."

The others had left.

Virgil and Josephine returned to Hell Canyon to a hero's

welcome. Josephine's animals accompanied them, with Stan leading the way. The men gathered around Virgil while the women gathered around Josephine. I heard a man congratulate Virgil as I joined the women.

"Congratulations Virgil, you caught the uncatchable bird."

Josephine's silhouette radiated the full spectrum of colors. A woman spoke.

"You look so happy."

Josephine's face beamed, just like it would in the earthly life. "I'm the luckiest woman in the world."

"How did it happen?"

Josephine held back. "It's kind of private."

"Come on."

Josephine's smile expanded. "He got me with poetry. I never had a chance."

Roland never recited poetry.

The men and women reunited. Josephine saw someone and waved a woman over. Then she did the same with Roland. I figured out her intentions and intervened.

"We talked about this, Josephine," Roland said.

"Lay off of my man," I yelled.

Everyone looked at me as Hell Canyon went silent. The woman's ivory silhouette put me in shock. It was Emily, the woman at my funeral. Her next six words sealed my fate.

"Martha, good to see you again."

Chapter 9

Josephine's face froze, and her mouth hung open. "What do you mean she's Martha?"

Emily's face looked tight, and her light flashed for a moment before it steadied. "That's what I've been trying to tell you, Madame Baker. The funeral was in progress when I arrived." She pointed at me. "She didn't arrive until after it ended and called herself Martha."

Josephine interrupted her and pointed at me. "And that's when she said she was looking for Dawn."

Emily's face relaxed. "*Oui Madame Baker, Oui.*"

A long silence followed. Josephine's face changed to a knife edge smile. "I've witnessed a lot of funerals since I passed through, but this is a first. Tell me why Dawn, that you believed it was important to attend your funeral under an alias."

I sensed everyone leaning in and understood why Norma and Patricia said to beware of her French friends. I needed an answer, but I didn't want to give them up. Fortunately, I found a lie.

"Some people who recently passed through said they heard rumors it was important to beware of your French friends. What was it they said? Oh yes, beware of what you and do and say?"

Some animals meowed, barked, or brayed, as Josephine's next words were so close to the truth that I almost confirmed it. "Probably those two stupid skanks, Norma and Patricia. Beware of my French friends, did they say that?"

Nobody said anything as my mouth kept its composure. "It

was a group of people who were by the river who said that. Like I said, it was just a rumor." Josephine looked me square in the eye and the smile sharpened. "Mess with them, and you're messing with me. Mess with me and you're messing with them. Do you get me?"

"Yes," I said in a soft voice.

She threw me a curve. "Do you know Mitch has been on my case about you?"

I recalled his perplexed look when I returned from my funeral.

"He doesn't think you attended your funeral. I had to tell him you snookered me into attending Hal's funeral and that Emily said you never showed. Do you know what happened next?"

I expected her to say that he fired her, but Josephine showed me it was much worse.

"He laughed at me, but it was a good joke even if it was at my expense. However, you made a fool of Roland, which I won't abide."

Roland had that shamed look of a man who thinks he should have known better. A wave of panic engulfed me. "Roland, I wouldn't do that," I said.

Roland didn't look at me.

Josephine's razor smile shifted. "Now this is what you're going to do. *You* are going to explain to the minutest detail to Roland why they laughed at your funeral. If you don't, then my French friends and I are going to do everything in our power to ensure you have a miserable eternal life. Now tell him the truth."

The humiliation would be too much if I told Roland everything, so I tried to tell him just enough to get by. However, Emily didn't let it happen.

"Madame Josephine, the people were laughing about a

eulogy delivered by a woman named Becky. They said she was Dawn's best friend."

Josephine's face lit up as her hue changed to blue and green. "Dawn, is this the same Becky who was showing your boyfriend a safe place to hide his sausage?"

I tried to deny it, but my body heat and my rosy glow gave me away. The crowd said, "Ohhhh."

Josephine's smile broadened. "Little girl, what did your best friend say at your funeral?" My body heat intensified.

"She talked about the time in high school where I made a boy buy tampons."

Josephine eyes opened and closed and her face twitched. "What?"

My rosy glow intensified. "That was Becky's eulogy."

Josephine's angry red color erupted. "You're setting off my BS detector." She turned on Emily. "What do you know about this?"

Snickers and muffled laughter squeezed out of the crowd.

Emily's face shrank, and her light flashed. "Madame Baker, I arrived too late for Becky's eulogy."

The silhouette of a donkey brayed as Josephine moved closer to me. "I'm trying to decide if you're messing with me, and I hope for your sake that you're not. Now, tell me everything about this woman's eulogy."

With a supreme effort, I steadied my silhouette. "It was about this boy in high school who liked me. His name was Kyle."

"Christ almighty, this better be good."

The crowd snickered some more.

Josephine scrutinized every word I uttered. "Kyle was an unattractive boy who asked me out."

"Where did you meet this boy?"

"It was a near a drugstore."

"Was Becky with you?"

"Yes, and it was her idea that he should buy the tampons."

Josephine stopped me again. "You went along with it."

My voice went weak. "Yes, I did."

She gave me a disgusted look. "Why did you want him to buy tampons?"

Shame spread across my face. "Becky challenged him to buy them if he wanted a date with me. We didn't think he would do it."

"No, you and Becky challenged him. Say it."

The rosy glow flushed my cheeks. "Becky and I challenged him."

"That's better. So he's in the drugstore. What happened next?"

Seeing Emily, the animals, and all of Hell Canyon watching me increased my body heat. "Kyle was trying to work up the nerve to buy a box when a clerk came up and told him to man up. He stole the box after the clerk left."

"Continue."

The rosy glow exploded as I concluded my confession. "A police officer saw Kyle make a run for the exit and gave chase. I left through the store's emergency exit."

Josephine eyes opened and closed for the longest time as she looked at me. Her mouth twitched intermittently. At last, she broke her silence and showed me my shame.

"Kyle may have been unattractive, but I'll give him one thing. He put himself out there. He chose to humiliate himself for you in front of your friend and the two of you treated him like three-fifths of a person."

The last time I heard those words was in Mr. Knoxville's

government class. I thought little about three-fifths back then but I understood it now as it stung my face. Josephine changed tack.

"How come Emily didn't see you?"

"I left after Becky's eulogy but changed my mind because my parents had not spoken but the funeral ended," I said.

Josephine's face brightened with understanding. "I get it. You left because Becky bruised your ego but then you returned."

Emily interrupted with words that carried an intense sting. "Her parents spoke. It was the usual boilerplate."

"Is there anything else?" Josephine asked.

Still suffering from Emily's words, my voice quietly said, "No."

Emily was not done. "Madam Josephine, the people at the funeral were laughing about a drunk flamingo."

Josephine's voice exploded as her color changed to an angry red, and the crowd laughed. "Please explain the drunk flamingo, Dawn."

The words flew out of my tongue. "I was wearing heels for the first time when Kyle saw me. Becky said I looked like a drunk flamingo."

The ferocity of her rage enveloped me. "I told you not to hold out on Roland."

Guilt shook my silhouette as the rosy glow burned deeper. "I didn't. I just couldn't remember it all."

Silence returned, and to my surprise, blue and green hues replaced Josephine's red and a smile formed.

"Let's summarize. A pimple-faced boy likes a girl who walks like a drunk flamingo. Pimple-face asks drunk flamingo for a date. Drunk flamingo isn't interested but lacks the nerve to tell him. So she hopes to fend him off by challenging him to buy her tampons but, to her dismay, he accepts her challenge. Pimple face works up enough nerve to get a box but not enough nerve to buy them. So he tries to steal them except a police officer catches him in the act while drunk flamingo flees through the back door."

The look on my face paid her off. Emily snickered, followed by the crowd's explosive laughter. A sound from Becky's eulogy replayed itself in my head.

"Wik-chuk, wik-chuk, wik-chuk, wik-chuk."

"Dawn, you did more than reimburse me. You made me a rich woman and I love those rosy cheeks," Josephine said while she and the crowd laughed. A man's voice rang out and silenced everyone. It was Mitch.

"Dawn, you're going to Ahwatukee to attend a wedding and you people will join her."

"Why are we attending a wedding?" someone asked.

"You've forgotten that our mission is to help people reconcile their earthly lives to their eternal lives."

Roland was missing.

***

We were at the top of 'Lamb of God' hill in Ahwatukee. The runners gave it that name because there was a church at the top of a long steep hill. I wondered what he had in mind as we floated among a parking lot full of cars. Josephine, Virgil, and everyone else had the same curious stare.

"Mitch, what are you doing?"

"It will become self-evident."

"What do you have in mind, Mitch?" Virgil asked.

Mitch expanded his voice and made eye contact with Josephine. "There's more to Dawn than you give her credit for. Now let's go to a wedding."

We entered through the walls, and he led me in front of the altar. Standing to one side was the minister and to my surprise, my ex-boyfriend Tom. Flanked on one side were the bridesmaids, all wearing pink dresses. On the opposite side were the groomsmen, all wearing tuxedos. A woman who looked familiar sat in the front row. I tried to remember who she was when, out of the corner of my eye, something in white appeared.

It was Becky, who wore a bridal gown of the most beautiful shade. A man in a tuxedo stood next to her. As they approached the altar, I understood the man was Mr. Darwin, her father, and the woman in the front row was Mrs. Darwin. They looked so much older. As they walked down the aisle, Becky had a slight curve. I suppressed my anger and spoke to Mitch under my breath.

"So you brought me to her wedding to finish me off."

"Give me a chance."

They stopped. Becky's father gave her a kiss, said something, and sat down with his wife as Becky proceeded the rest of the way. The music ceased, and the ceremony began. Mitch spoke again. "Soon, Becky will speak to you."

Mitch continued to baffle me." What, literally speak to me, but she's in the earthly life."

"It will become clear in just a moment."

"The bride will now give a tribute in remembrance of her best friend," the minister said, as if on cue.

"Okay, Dawn, pay attention," Mitch said.

A bridesmaid gave Becky a sealed envelope, which she opened. Becky removed a sheet of paper and returned the opened envelope to the bridesmaid, who then returned to her position. Becky checked her posture, looked at the crowd, then to the sheet, and spoke.

"I must tell you about a special woman named Dawn Allegary. She was the best friend that I ever had. We met in the first grade, helped each other with class work and did fun things, but occasionally we got into trouble."

"When we were in fourth grade, we heard a rumor that black ink would squirt out of the hallway fire alarm if you pulled it and we wanted to see if it was true."

The audience interrupted with a laugh. "We used an eighteen-inch ruler to flick the lever open. Dawn worked the ruler while I kept a lookout for anyone coming down the hall. It was taking forever, and Dawn worried about the ink staining her clothes. Finally, she got the lever down. No ink squirted out of the hole, but the alarm sure made a loud noise."

The crowd laughed some more.

"We ran. I got away, but a teacher caught her and took her to the Principal's office. I was sure that would be my fate, except it was not because she did not give me up."

Becky's lip trembled. She paused and took a deep breath.

"Our friendship matured when we reached high school and we still found trouble but she always remained my friend."

Her eyes fluttered as she pointed to the groom, and she gritted her teeth for a moment before speaking. "This man was her ex-boyfriend and their love was coming together when the lightning bolt struck her down. We met at her funeral and had coffee afterward, and to my surprise, I found love. So in her death she gave me new life and..." Becky wept and her knees buckled as Tom grabbed her. "I should have given her a better eulogy."

The minister took the paper from her hand and finished reciting what she wrote as Tom held her close. "So in her death she gave me new life and the chance to be the happiest woman on earth. Now, to honor what she gave, I will name my child after her. Dawn, you may not have known how to play the game, but you had a big heart, which I didn't deserve. Take care until we meet again."

I felt the tears' weight on my words. "Don't worry, Becky. It's all good."

"Looks like you made good on your first chance," Mitch said.

"How did you know?"

"One of Josephine's friends told me."

I could think of only one person who could have told him, but I couldn't be sure, Emily.

Mrs. Darwin stepped up to the altar with purse in hand, gently eased Becky from Tom's grasp and looked in her face. Becky's mascara had smeared. "I miss Dawn too," she said. Then she turned to the bridesmaids. "Does anyone have a bottle of water?"

All of them quickly looked around. One of them saw a bottle and gave it to her.

Mrs. Darwin reached into her purse and pulled out some paper tissues. "Wet these tissues," she said to the nearest bridesmaid. She did so.

"The last time I cleaned your face you were four years old. You ate a peanut butter and jelly sandwich. I don't know what happened to the peanut butter, but the jelly was all over you."

"It was grape jelly." Becky smiled. The groomsmen, bridesmaids, and I also smiled.

The wedding proceeded, and Mitch surprised me again.

"You need to thank Josephine."

Red color flared my silhouette. "Her, the one that tells my boyfriend I'm no good." Concern for Roland flared up.

"She found you."

My conscience told me Mitch was right. "Okay, I'll do it."

"Make sure your words are real."

Josephine was holding Virgil's hand as I heard the groom give his vow. I searched for the words to express my gratitude but thank you wouldn't cut it; the currency was too cheap. Then out of nowhere the words came, which I said while averting my eyes.

"Lieutenant Josephine, may I ask you a question?"

Her silhouette jerked, but her voice was sunny. "Go ahead, what is your question?"

"Is this a good wedding?"

"Yes, yes, it is Private. It's a very good wedding."

The next words I said tasted like spoiled food. "By the way, thanks for finding me."

She nodded, and I assumed she accepted my payment. I returned to Mitch, who expected my question.

"You don't want to have eternal enemies."

The minister's next words caught my attention. "This couple found seeds of love in death's despair. They planted the seeds into the other and nurtured them until they grew into trees of life. Now they come before us to merge their two separate trees into one tree of partnership."

Thoughts of Roland plagued me as the wedding proceeded. I was about to ask Mitch where he might be when two silhouettes with splintered lights appeared. It was Hal and a girl, and they rushed to Virgil.

"Virgil, I found out why I killed myself," Hal exclaimed.

"Let's go outside," Virgil replied, and they left.

"You may kiss the bride," the minister announced. The audiences, both earthly and eternal, cheered.

The people filed out of the church full of cheerful words and drove away. Mitch was talking to another man nearby, while Norma and Patricia were chatting with some men and women in the parking lot. Hal and the girl left Virgil and approached.

Hal had the bright look of a redeemed man. "Dawn, I'm so glad to see you again. This is my girl, Crissa."

Crissa squeezed Hal's hand. "Pleased to meet you. He's told me how you looked out for him."

I concealed my surprise. "We were in a tough spot."

Hal's face brightened. "A man told us faith is believing you'll see the daylight no matter how strong the darkness."

"And you killed yourself because you did not believe you would see the daylight," I said.

Crissa squeezed Hal's hand again. "It's why *we* killed ourselves."

"We understand now what the issue was. We wish we had known it in our earthly lives," Hal said.

I paid them a compliment. "Well, you're giving each other daylight and that's a start."

Crissa wrapped her arms around Hal's chest, showing a man whose silhouette stood tall and proud, a man with purpose.

Hal said he met Crissa and soon after he joined his new friends, and fell for each other. They had good times, but he and Crissa discovered they couldn't stay.

"The problems we had in the earthly life followed us into the eternal life," Hal said.

"We had to face up to ourselves," Crissa said.

Hal and Crissa planned to build a life together to show their loved ones they made good. They called it their House of Penance, but they needed Virgil's guidance. Hal's silhouette shook when he voiced his deepest fear. "Virgil agreed to help us, but I don't know if it will be good enough to square it with Mom."

Could the House of Penance heal the woman with the face of broken glass?

The words from a voice I did not want to hear accosted me. "Hey drunk flamingo, I've got good news."

I exhaled resignation. "What's your good news, Josephine?"

"Your granny's coming to Hell Canyon in two days."

Mitch's voice thundered. "You better not be joking."

"It's the real deal."

My voice cracked, accompanied by heartache. "I'm meeting my grandmother?"

"Annabelle Thorson, right?"

Hearing her name increased the heartache. Could Josephine have found what I lost? Guilt about Kyle intruded. "That's her but I don't deserve it."

"You don't, but she does. What a wonderful woman."

"Josephine!" Mitch exclaimed.

"Okay, you do." Josephine returned to Virgil.

"That's splendid news," Crissa said.

Roland appeared, emitting shades of red and purple. My heart quaked. "Roland, where have you been?"

Roland glared at me. "You made a fool out of me, Dawn."

My lips trembled. "I didn't mean to."

His colors became harsh. "So you wanted to travel to hide the truth about yourself."

Tears fell. "I didn't want you to see the ugly parts of me. You deserve only the good parts."

Roland's delivered his next words with lethal smoothness. "They say women find themselves attracted to certain men because they have qualities they lack in themselves."

"That's true."

Roland reduced to me to road kill before he left. "You lack

honesty. We're done."

Norma and Patricia approached and finished me off. "You built up a man's heart only to destroy it utterly and completely. Girl, you have potential. We'll see you after this is over," Norma said.

Mitch was about to say something when Patricia cut him off. "Don't go there, you hypocrite."

"Get out of here," Crissa yelled.

"You heard her, go," Hal said.

They left with a smile, and I remembered the first time they looked at Hal. Mitch approached as wounded words limped out of my heart. "I made good on my first chance, but I blew my second chance."

A familiar voice from Omaha intervened. "It's not over yet." It was Ester.

Chapter 10

"You tried to run from your past," Ester said.

I admitted I did.

"The past always catches you."

Ester told me to wait for a week before returning to Omaha while she talked to Roland. I agreed and the chance to reunite with Grandma made my heart pound. Before leaving, she gave me some advice.

"Remember, when I told you about the equations of love and hate. You need to choose carefully."

I nodded.

"I chose equations of love and my enemy became my lover, but don't worry. You don't have to kiss Josephine."

I laughed.

"One last piece of advice before I go."

"What's that?"

"Next time, buy your own tampons."

Words could not describe the emotions I felt when I saw grandma. Her ivory silhouette shined blue and green when she said, "Hi Dawn, good to see you again." What I lost on 13 June 1992 was found. She periodically followed my earthly life and said my running store would have been a good one. Grandma told me she settled on Victoria Island in Canada, told me to visit, and she would reunite me with our other relations.

I thought about the woman who made this possible. She destroyed me utterly and completely, only to build me up. Who are you, Josephine Baker?

Ester told me Roland was at the Harry A. Burke High School. She said two words before I left the museum: Be true. Roland was there watching the students.

"Hi," I said.

He didn't look at me. "Hi."

Sure that I had lost him, I decided to speak my last words and leave. "The biggest mistake I made in the earthly life was treating Kyle like a three-fifths a person. The biggest mistake I made in the eternal life was giving you only three-fifths of me."

Roland stirred, but said nothing.

I held back tears when I recalled Hal's definition of faith. "Hal said faith is believing in the daylight no matter how strong the darkness. I need your daylight."

Roland's next words surprised me. "You're lucky I can't get enough of your dazzling light."

My silhouette trembled as I said nothing.

"Becky was right. You have a big heart, which I saw you give to Giles."

All I could say was thanks. Roland came close. "Do you still want to go to Paris?"

I nodded as he took my hand.

"We'll take the long away. Follow me."

Surprise, fear, and excitement swirled within me as Roland took me straight up. We passed the clouds and still he kept going.

"Roland, where are you taking me?"

"We're almost there."

We stopped, and he said, "We're at low-earth orbit."

What I saw took away my breath.

Lightning streaked out of clouds, which partially covered oceans. South America divided the Pacific on the left and the

Atlantic on the right.

"Look up," Roland said.

An infinity of stars spread themselves through an eternity of space. The magnitude of creation humbled me. "It's amazing," I said.

"I came up here by myself once, but it was too lonely. It's much better with someone else."

A warm rush passed through me. I turned to look at him and found him looking at me.

"We need to do one more thing."

"What's that?"

He put a finger just below my neck. "Kiss and make up."

My silhouette warmed into a flame. His finger descended and my shade vanished, revealing me in full. Roland spoke again.

"Don't you think we should kiss and make up?"

My voice stuttered as I displayed all my light. "Yes."

The flame intensified when he wrapped his arms around my waist, showed his eyes, and said five magic words.

"Let me touch your light."

I kissed the man and began my eternal life.

The End

To Crissa, may God give you a second chance

Printed in the USA
CPSIA information can be obtained
at www.ICGtesting.com
LVHW041734060823
754339LV00002B/257

9 781804 390566